The Mistress of Shenstone

Florence L. Barclay

The Mistress of Shenstone

The present edition is a reproduction of previous publication of this classic work. Minor typographical errors may have been corrected without note; however, for an authentic reading experience the spelling, punctuation, and capitalization have been retained from the original text.

ISBN: 978-1-64799-965-0

To

C. W. B.

CONTENTS

THE MISTRESS OF SHENSTONE

CHAPTER I

ON THE TERRACE AT SHENSTONE

Three o'clock on a dank afternoon, early in November. The wintry sunshine, in fitful gleams, pierced the greyness of the leaden sky.

The great trees in Shenstone Park stood gaunt and bare, spreading wide arms over the sodden grass. All nature seemed waiting the first fall of winter's snow, which should hide its deadness and decay under a lovely pall of sparkling white, beneath which a promise of fresh life to come might gently move and stir; and, eventually, spring forth.

The Mistress of Shenstone moved slowly up and down the terrace, wrapped in her long cloak, listening to the soft "drip, drip" of autumn all around; noting the silent fall of the last dead leaves; the steely grey of the lake beyond; the empty flower-garden; the deserted lawn.

The large stone house had a desolate appearance, most of the rooms being, evidently, closed; but, in one or two, cheerful log-fires blazed, casting a ruddy glow upon the window-panes, and sending forth a tempting promise of warmth and cosiness within.

A tiny white toy-poodle walked the terrace with his mistress— an agitated little bundle of white curls; sometimes running round and round her; then hurrying on before, or dropping behind, only to rush on, in unexpected haste, at the corners; almost tripping her up, as she turned.

"Peter," said Lady Ingleby, on one of these occasions, "I do wish you would behave in a more rational manner! Either come to heel and follow sedately, as a dog of your age should do; or trot on in front, in the gaily juvenile manner you assume when Michael takes you out for a walk; but, for goodness sake, don't be so fidgety; and don't run round and round me in this bewildering way, or I shall call for William, and send you in. I only wish Michael could see you!"

1

The little animal looked up at her, pathetically, through his tumbled curls—a soft silky mass, which had earned for him his name of Shockheaded Peter. His eyes, red-rimmed from the cold wind, had that unseeing look, often noticeable in a very old dog. Yet there was in them, and in the whole pose of his tiny body, an anguish of anxiety, which could not have escaped a genuine dog-lover. Even Lady Ingleby became partially aware of it. She stooped and patted his head.

"Poor little Peter," she said, more kindly. "It is horrid, for us both, having Michael so far away at this tiresome war. But he will come home before long; and we shall forget all the anxiety and loneliness. It will be spring again. Michael will have you properly clipped, and we will go to Brighton, where you enjoy trotting about, and hearing people call you 'The British Lion.' I verily believe you consider yourself the size of the lions in Trafalgar Square! I cannot imagine why a great big man, such as Michael, is so devoted to a tiny scrap of a dog, such as you! Now, if you were a Great Dane, or a mighty St. Bernard—! However, Michael loves us both, and we both love Michael; so we must be nice to each other, little Peter, while he is away."

Myra Ingleby smiled, drew the folds of her cloak more closely around her, and moved on. A small white shadow, with no wag to its tail, followed dejectedly behind.

And the dead leaves, loosing their hold of the sapless branches, fluttered to the sodden turf; and the soft "drip, drip" of autumn fell all around.

The door of the lower hall opened. A footman, bringing a telegram, came quickly out. His features were set, in well-trained impassivity; but his eyelids flickered nervously as he handed the silver salver to his mistress.

Lady Ingleby's lovely face paled to absolute whiteness beneath her large beaver hat; but she took up the orange envelope with a steady hand, opening it with fingers which did not tremble. As she glanced at the signature, the colour came back to her cheeks.

"From Dr. Brand," she said, with an involuntary exclamation of relief; and the waiting footman turned and nodded furtively toward the house. A maid, at a window, dropped the blind, and ran to tell the anxious household all was well.

Meanwhile, Lady Ingleby read her telegram.

Visiting patient in your neighbourhood. Can you put me up for the night? Arriving 4.30.

Deryck Brand.

2

Lady Ingleby turned to the footman. "William," she said, "tell Mrs. Jarvis, Sir Deryck Brand is called to this neighbourhood, and will stay here to-night. They can light a fire at once in the magnolia room, and prepare it for him. He will be here in an hour. Send the motor to the station. Tell Groatley we will have tea in my sitting-room as soon as Sir Deryck arrives. Send down word to the Lodge to Mrs. O'Mara, that I shall want her up here this evening. Oh, and—by the way—mention at once at the Lodge that there is no further news from abroad."

"Yes, m' lady," said the footman; and Myra Ingleby smiled at the reflection, in the lad's voice and face, of her own immense relief. He turned and hastened to the house; Peter, in a sudden access of misplaced energy, barking furiously at his heels.

Lady Ingleby moved to the front of the terrace and stood beside one of the stone lions, close to an empty vase, which in summer had been a brilliant mass of scarlet geraniums. Her face was glad with expectation.

"Somebody to talk to, at last!" she said. "I had begun to think I should have to brave dear mamma, and return to town. And Sir Deryck of all people! He wires from Victoria, so I conclude he sees his patient en route, or in the morning. How perfectly charming of him to give me a whole evening. I wonder how many people would, if they knew of it, be breaking the tenth commandment concerning me! ... Peter, you little fiend! Come here! Why the footmen, and gardeners, and postmen, do not kick out your few remaining teeth, passes me! You pretend to be too unwell to eat your dinner, and then behave like a frantic hyena, because poor innocent William brings me a telegram! I shall write and ask Michael if I may have you hanged."

And, in high good humour, Lady Ingleby went into the house.

But, outside, the dead leaves turned slowly, and rustled on the grass; while the soft "drip, drip" of autumn fell all around. The dying year was almost dead; and nature waited for her pall of snow.

CHAPTER II

THE FORERUNNER

"What it is to have somebody to talk to, at last! And you, of all people, dear Doctor! Though I still fail to understand how a patient, who has brought you down to these parts, can wait for your visit until to-morrow morning, thus giving a perfectly healthy person, such as myself, the inestimable privilege of your company at tea, dinner, and breakfast, with delightful tête-à-têtes in between. All the world knows your minutes are golden."

Thus Lady Ingleby, as she poured out the doctor's tea, and handed it to him.

Deryck Brand placed the cup carefully on his corner of the folding tea-table, helped himself to thin bread-and-butter; then answered, with his most charming smile,

"Mine would be a very dismal profession dear lady, if it precluded me from ever having a meal, or a conversation, or from spending a pleasant evening, with a perfectly healthy person. I find the surest way to live one's life to the full, accomplishing the maximum amount of work with the minimum amount of strain, is to cultivate the habit of living in the present; giving the whole mind to the scene, the subject, the person, of the moment. Therefore, with your leave, we will dismiss my patients, past and future; and enjoy, to the full, this unexpected tête-à-tête."

Myra Ingleby looked at her visitor. His forty-two years sat lightly on him, notwithstanding the streaks of silver in the dark hair just over each temple. There was a youthful alertness about the tall athletic figure; but the lean brown face, clean shaven and reposeful, held a look of quiet strength and power, mingled with a keen kindliness and ready comprehension, which inspired trust, and drew forth confidence.

The burden of a great loneliness seemed lifted from Myra's heart.

"Do you always put so much salt on your bread-and-butter?" she said. "And how glad I am to be 'the person of the moment.' Only—until this mysterious 'patient in the neighbourhood' demands your attention,—you ought to be having a complete holiday, and I must try to forget that I am talking to the greatest nerve specialist of the day, and only realise the pleasure of entertaining so good a friend of Michael's and my own. Otherwise I should be tempted to

4

consult you; for I really believe, Sir Deryck, for the first time in my life, I am becoming neurotic."

The doctor did not need to look at his hostess. His practised eye had already noted the thin cheeks; the haunted look; the purple shadows beneath the lovely grey eyes, for which the dark fringes of black eyelashes were not altogether accountable. He leaned forward and looked into the fire.

"If such is really the case," he said, "that you should be aware of it, is so excellent a symptom, that the condition cannot be serious. But I want you to remember, Lady Ingleby, that I count all my patients, friends; also that my friends may consider themselves at liberty, at any moment, to become my patients. So consult me, if I can be of any use to you."

The doctor helped himself to more bread-and-butter, folding it with careful precision.

Lady Ingleby held out her hand for his cup, grateful that he did not appear to notice the rush of unexpected tears to her eyes. She busied herself with the urn until she could control her voice; then said, with a rather tremulous laugh: "Ah, thank you! Presently—if I may—I gladly will consult you. Meanwhile, how do you like 'the scene of the moment'? Do you consider my boudoir improved? Michael made all these alterations before he went away. The new electric lights are a patent arrangement of his own. And had you seen his portrait? A wonderful likeness, isn't it?"

The doctor looked around him, appreciatively.

"I have been admiring the room, ever since I entered," he said. "It is charming." Then he raised his eyes to the picture over the mantelpiece:—the life-sized portrait of a tall, bearded man, with the high brow of the scholar and thinker; the eyes of the mystic; the gentle unruffled expression of the saint. He appeared old enough to be the father of the woman in whose boudoir his portrait was the central object. The artist had painted him in an old Norfolk shooting-suit, leather leggings, hunting-crop in hand, seated in a garden chair, beside a rustic table. Everything in the picture was homely, old, and comfortable; the creases in the suit were old friends; the ancient tobacco pouch on the table was worn and stained. Russet-brown predominated, and the highest light in the painting was the clear blue of those dreamy, musing eyes. They were bent upon the table, where sat, in an expectant attitude of adoring attention, a white toy-poodle. The palpable devotion between the big man and the tiny dog, the concentrated affection with which they looked at one another, were very cleverly depicted. The picture might have been called: "We two"; also it left an impression of a friendship in which there had been no room for a third. The doctor

5

glanced, for an instant, at the lovely woman on the lounge, behind the silver urn, and his subconsciousness propounded the question: "Where did she come in?" But the next moment he turned towards the large armchair on his right, where a small dejected mass of white curls lay in a huddled heap. It was impossible to distinguish between head and tail.

"Is this the little dog?" asked the doctor.

"Yes; that is Peter. But in the picture he is smart and properly clipped, and feeling better than he does just now. Peter and Michael are devoted to each other; and, when Michael is away, Peter is left in my charge. But I am not fond of small dogs; and I really consider Peter very much spoilt. Also I always feel he just tolerates me because I am Michael's wife, and remains with me because, where I am, there Michael will return. But I am quite kind to him, for Michael's sake. Only he really is a nasty little dog; and too old to be allowed to continue. Michael always speaks of him as if he were quite too good to live; and, personally, I think it is high time he went where all good dogs go. I cannot imagine what is the matter with him now. Since yesterday afternoon he has refused all his food, and been so restless and fidgety. He always sleeps on Michael's bed; and, as a rule, after I have put him there, and closed the door between Michael's room and mine, I hear no more of Peter, until he barks to be let out in the morning, and my maid takes him downstairs. But last night, he whined and howled for hours. At length I got up, found Michael's old shooting jacket—the very one in the portrait—and laid it on the bed. Peter crawled into it, and cuddled down, I folded the sleeves around him, and he seemed content. But to-day he still refuses to eat. I believe he is dyspeptic, or has some other complaint, such as dogs develop when they are old. Honestly—don't you think—a little effective poison, in an attractive pill——?"

"Oh, hush!" said the doctor. "Peter may not be asleep."

Lady Ingleby laughed. "My dear Sir Deryck! Do you suppose animals understand our conversation?"

"Indeed I do," replied the doctor. "And more than that, they do not require the medium of language. Their comprehension is telepathic. They read our thoughts. A nervous rider or driver can terrify a horse. Dumb creatures will turn away from those who think of them with dislike or aversion; whereas a true lover of animals can win them without a spoken word. The thought of love and of goodwill reaches them telepathically, winning instant trust and response. Also, if we take the trouble to do so, we can, to a great extent, arrive at their ideas, in the same way."

"Extraordinary!" exclaimed Lady Ingleby. "Well, I wish you

6

would thought-read what is the matter with Peter. I shall not know how to face Michael's home-coming, if anything goes wrong with his belovèd dog."

The doctor lay back in his armchair; crossed his knees the one over the other; rested his elbows on the arms of the chair; then let his finger-tips meet very exactly. Instinctively he assumed the attitude in which he usually sat when bending his mind intently on a patient. Presently he turned and looked steadily at the little white heap curled up in the big armchair.

The room was very still.

"Peter!" said the doctor, suddenly.

Peter sat up at once, and peeped at the doctor, through his curls.

"Poor little Peter," said the doctor, kindly.

Peter moved to the edge of the chair; sat very upright, and looked eagerly across to where the doctor was sitting. Then he wagged his tail, tapping the chair with quick, anxious, little taps.

"The first wag I have seen in twenty-four hours," remarked Lady Ingleby; but neither Deryck Brand nor Shockheaded Peter heeded the remark.

The anxious eyes of the dog were gazing, with an agony of question, into the kind keen eyes of the man.

Without moving, the doctor spoke.

"Yes, little Peter," he said.

Peter's small tufted tail ceased thumping. He sat very still for a moment; then quietly moved back to the middle of the chair, turned round and round three or four times; then lay down, dropping his head between his paws with one long shuddering sigh, like a little child which has sobbed itself to sleep.

The doctor turned, and looked at Lady Ingleby.

"What does that mean?" queried Myra, astonished.

"Little Peter asked a question," replied Sir Deryck, gravely; "and I answered it."

"Wonderful! Will you talk this telepathy over with Michael when he comes home? It would interest him."

The doctor looked into the fire.

"It is a big subject," he said. "When I can spare the time, I am thinking of writing an essay on the mental and spiritual development of animals, as revealed in the Bible."

"Balaam's ass?" suggested Lady Ingleby, promptly.

The doctor smiled. "Quite so," he said. "But Balaam's ass is neither the only animal in the Bible, nor the most interesting case. Have you ever noticed the many instances in which animals immediately obeyed God's commands, even when those commands

7

ran counter to their strongest instincts? For instance:—the lion, who met the disobedient man of God on the road from Bethel. The instinct of the beast, after slaying the man, would have been to maul the body, drag it away into his lair, and devour it. But the Divine command was:—that he should slay, but not eat the carcass, nor tear the ass. The instinct of the ass would have been to flee in terror from the lion; but, undoubtedly, a Divine assurance overcame her natural fear; and all men who passed by beheld this remarkable sight:—a lion and an ass standing sentry, one on either side of the dead body of the man of God; and there they remained until the old prophet from Bethel arrived, to fetch away the body and bury it."

"Extraordinary!" said Lady Ingleby. "So they did. And now one comes to think of it there are plenty of similar instances. The instinct of the serpent which Moses lifted up on a pole, would have been to come scriggling down, and go about biting the Israelites, instead of staying up on the pole, to be looked at for their healing."

The doctor smiled. "Quite so," he said, "Only, we must not quote him as an instance; because, being made of brass, I fear he was devoid of instinct. Otherwise he would have been an excellent case in point. And I believe animals possess far more spiritual life than we suspect. Do you remember a passage in the Psalms which says that the lions 'seek their meat from God'? And, more striking still, in the same Psalm we read of the whole brute creation, that when God hides His face 'they are troubled.' Good heavens!" said the doctor, earnestly; "I wish our spiritual life always answered to these two tests:—that God's will should be paramount over our strongest instincts; and that any cloud between us and the light of His face, should cause us instant trouble of soul."

"I like that expression 'spiritual life,'" said Lady Ingleby. "I am sure you mean by it what other people sometimes express so differently. Did you hear of the Duchess of Meldrum attending that big evangelistic meeting in the Albert Hall? I really don't know exactly what it was. Some sort of non-sectarian mission, I gather, with a preacher over from America; and the meetings went on for a fortnight. It would never have occurred to me to go to them. But the dear old duchess always likes to be 'in the know' and to sample everything. Besides, she holds a proprietary stall. So she sailed into the Albert Hall one afternoon, in excellent time, and remained throughout the entire proceedings. She enjoyed the singing; thought the vast listening crowd, marvellous; was moved to tears by the eloquence of the preacher, and was leaving the hall more touched than she had been for years, and fully intending to return, bringing others with her, when a smug person, hovering about the entrance, accosted her with: 'Excuse me madam; are you a Christian?' The duchess raised her lorgnette in blank amazement, and looked him tip and down. Very likely the tears still glistened upon her proud old face. Anyway this impossible person appears to have considered her a promising case. Emboldened by her silence, he laid his hand upon her arm, and repeated his question: 'Madam, are you a Christian?' Then the duchess awoke to the situation with a vengeance. 'My good man,' she said, clearly and deliberately, so that all in the lobby could hear; 'I should have thought it would have been perfectly patent to your finely trained perceptions, that I am an engaging mixture of Jew, Turk, Infidel, and Heathen Chinee! Now, if you will kindly stand aside, I will pass to my carriage.'—And the duchess sampled no more evangelistic meetings!"

The doctor sighed. "Tactless," he said. "Ah, the pity of it, when 'fools rush in where angels fear to tread!'"

"People scream with laughter, when the duchess tells it," said Lady Ingleby; "but then she imitates the unctuous person so exactly; and she does not mention the tears. I have them from an eye-witness. But—as I was saying—I like your expression: 'spiritual life.' It really holds a meaning; and, though one may have to admit one does not possess any, or, that what one does possess is at a low ebb, yet one sees the genuine thing in others, and it is something to believe in, at all events.—Look how peacefully little Peter is sleeping. You have evidently set his mind at rest. That is Michael's armchair; and, therefore, Peter's. Now we will send away the tea-things; and then—may I become a patient?"

CHAPTER III

WHAT PETER KNEW

"Isn't my good Groatley a curious looking person?" said Lady Ingleby, as the door closed behind the butler. "I call him the Gryphon, because he looks perpetually astonished. His eyebrows are like black horseshoes, and they mount higher and higher up his forehead as one's sentence proceeds. But he is very faithful, and knows his work, and Michael approves him. Do you like this portrait of Michael? Garth Dalmain stayed here a few months before he lost his sight, poor boy, and painted us both. I believe mine was practically his last portrait. It hangs in the dining-room."

The doctor moved his chair opposite the fireplace, so that he could sit facing the picture over the mantelpiece, yet turn readily toward Lady Ingleby on his left. On his right, little Peter, with an occasional sobbing sigh, slept heavily in his absent master's chair. The log-fire burned brightly. The electric light, from behind amber glass, sent a golden glow as of sunshine through the room. The dank damp drip of autumn had no place in this warm luxury. The curtains were closely drawn; and that which is not seen, can be forgotten.

The doctor glanced at the clock. The minute-hand pointed to the quarter before six.

He lifted his eyes to the picture.

"I hardly know Lord Ingleby sufficiently well to give an opinion; but I should say it is an excellent likeness, possessing, to a large degree, the peculiar quality of all Dalmain's portraits:—the more you look at them, the more you see in them. They are such extraordinary character studies. With your increased knowledge of the person, grows your appreciation of the cleverness of the portrait."

"Yes," said Lady Ingleby, leaning forward to look intently up at the picture. "It often startles me as I come into the room, because I see a fresh expression on the face, just according to my own mood, or what I happen to have been doing; and I realise Michael's mind on the subject more readily from the portrait than from my own knowledge of him. Garth Dalmain was a genius!"

"Now tell me," said the doctor, gently. "Why did you leave town, your many friends, your interests there, in order to bury yourself down here, during this dismal autumn weather? Surely the strain of waiting for news would have been less, within such easy reach of the War Office and of the evening papers."

Lady Ingleby laughed, rather mirthlessly.

"I came away, Sir Deryck, partly to escape from dear mamma; and as you do not know dear mamma, it is almost impossible for you to understand how essential it was to escape. When Michael is away, I am defenceless. Mamma swoops down; takes up her abode in my house; reduces my household, according to their sex and temperament, to rage, hysterics, or despair; tells unpalatable home-truths to my friends, so that all—save the duchess—flee discomforted. Then mamma proceeds to 'divide the spoil'! In other words: she lies in wait for my telegrams, and opens them herself, saying that if they contain good news, a dutiful daughter should delight in at once sharing it with her; whereas, if they contain bad news, which heaven forbid!—and surely, with mamma snorting skyward, heaven would not venture to do otherwise!—she is the right person to break it to me, gently. I bore it for six weeks; then fled down here, well knowing that not even the dear delight of bullying me would bring mamma to Shenstone in autumn."

The doctor's face was grave. For a moment he looked silently into the fire. He was a man of many ideals, and foremost among them was his ideal of the relation which should be between parents and children; of the loyalty to a mother, which, even if forced to admit faults or failings, should tenderly shield them from the knowledge or criticism of outsiders. It hurt him, as a sacrilege, to hear a daughter speak thus of her mother; yet he knew well, from facts which were common knowledge, how little cause the sweet, lovable woman at his side had to consider the tie either a sacred or a tender one. He had come to help, not to find fault. Also, the minute-hand was hastening towards the hour; and the final instructions of the kind-hearted old Duchess of Meldrum, as she parted from him at the War Office, had been: "Remember! Six o'clock from London. I shall insist upon its being kept back until then. If they make difficulties, I shall camp in the entrance and 'hold up' every messenger who attempts to pass out. But I am accustomed to have my own way with these good people. I should not hesitate to ring up Buckingham Palace, if necessary, as they very well know! So you may rest assured it will not leave London until six o'clock. It gives you ample time."

Therefore the doctor said: "I understand. It does not come within my own experience; yet I think I understand. But tell me, Lady Ingleby. If bad news were to come, would you sooner receive it direct from the War Office, in the terribly crude wording which

11

cannot be avoided in those telegrams; or would you rather that a friend—other than your mother—broke it to you, more gently?"

Myra's eyes flashed. She sat up with instant animation.

"Oh, I would receive it direct," she said. "It would be far less hard, if it were official. I should hear the roll of the drums, and see the wave of the flag. For England, and for Honour! A soldier's daughter, and a soldier's wife, should be able to stand up to anything. If they had to tell me Michael was in great danger, I should share his danger in receiving the news without flinching. If he were wounded, as I read the telegram I should receive a wound myself, and try to be as brave as he. All which came direct from the war, would unite me to Michael. But interfering friends, however well-meaning, would come between. If he had not been shielded from a bullet or a sword-thrust, why should I be shielded from the knowledge of his wound?"

The doctor screened his face with his hand,

"I see," he said.

The clock struck six.

"But that was not the only reason I left town," continued Lady Ingleby, with evident effort. Then she flung out both hands towards him. "Oh, doctor! I wonder if I might tell you a thing which has been a burden on my heart and life for years!"

There followed a tense moment of silence; but the doctor was used to such moments, and could usually determine during the silence, whether the confidence should be allowed or avoided. He turned and looked steadily at the lovely wistful face.

It was the face of an exceedingly beautiful woman, nearing thirty. But the lovely eyes still held the clear candour of the eyes of a little child, the sweet lips quivered with quickly felt emotion, the low brow showed no trace of shame or sin. The doctor knew he was in the presence of one of the most popular hostesses, one of the most admired women, in the kingdom. Yet his keen professional insight revealed to him an arrested development; possibilities unfulfilled; a problem of inadequacy and consequent disappointment, to which he had not the key. But those outstretched hands eagerly held it towards him. Could he bring help, if he accepted a knowledge of the solution; or—did help come too late?

"Dear Lady Ingleby," he said, quietly; "tell me anything you like; that is to say, anything which you feel assured Lord Ingleby would allow discussed with a third person."

Myra leaned back among the cushions and laughed—a gay little laugh, half of amusement, half of relief.

"Oh, Michael would not mind!" she said. "Anything Michael would mind, I have always told straight to himself; and they were

12

silly little things; such as foolish people trying to make love to me; or a foreign prince, with moustaches like the German Emperor's, offering to shoot Michael, if I would promise to marry him when his period of consequent imprisonment was over. I cut the idiots who had presumed to make love to me, ever after; and assured the foreign prince, I should undoubtedly kill him myself, if he hurt a hair of Michael's head! No, dear doctor. My life is clear of all that sort of complication. My trouble is a harder one, involving one's whole life-problem. And that problem is incompetence and inadequacy—not towards the world, I should not care a rap for that; but towards the one to whom I owe most: towards Michael,—my husband."

The doctor moved uneasily in his chair, and glanced at the clock.

"Oh, hush!" he said. "Do not——"

"No!" cried Myra. "You must not stop me. Let me at last have the relief of speech! My friend, I am twenty-eight; I have had ten years of married life; yet I do not believe I have ever really grown up! In heart and brain I am an undeveloped child, and I know it; and, worse still, Michael knows it, and—Michael does not mind. Listen! It dates back to years ago. Mamma never allowed any of her daughters to grow up. We were permitted no individuality of our own, no opinions, no independence. All that was required of us, was to 'do her behests, and follow in her train.' Forgive the misquotation. We were always children in mamma's eyes. We grew tall; we grew good-looking; but we never grew up. We remained children, to be snubbed, domineered over, and bullied. My sisters, who were good children, had plenty of jam and cake; and, eventually, husbands after mamma's own heart were found for them. Perhaps you know how those marriages have turned out?"

Lady Ingleby paused, and the doctor made an almost imperceptible sign of assent. One of the ladies in question, a most unhappy woman, was under treatment in his Mental Sanatorium at that very moment; but he doubted whether Lady Ingleby knew it.

"I was the black sheep," continued Myra, finding no remark forthcoming. "Nothing I did was ever right; everything I did was always wrong. When Michael met me I was nearly eighteen, the height I am now, but in the nursery, as regards mental development or knowledge of the world; and, as regards character, a most unhappy, utterly reckless, little child. Michael's love, when at last I realised it, was wonderful to me. Tenderness, appreciation, consideration, were experiences so novel that they would have turned my head, had not the elation they produced been counterbalanced by a gratitude which was overwhelming; and a

13

terror of being handed back to mamma, which would have made me agree to anything. Years later, Michael told me that what first attracted him to me was a look in my eyes just like the look in those of a favourite spaniel of his, who was always in trouble with everyone else, and had just been accidentally shot, by a keeper. Michael told me this himself; and really thought I should be pleased! Somehow it gave me the key to my standing with him—just that of a very tenderly-loved pet dog. No words can say how good he has always been to me. If I lost him, I should lose my all—everything which makes home, home; and life a safe, and certain, thing. But if he lost little Peter, it would be a more real loss to him than if he lost me; because Peter is more intelligent for his size, and really more of an actual companion to Michael, than I am. Many a time, when he has passed through my room on the way to his, with Peter tucked securely under his arm; and saying, 'Good-night, my dear,' to me, has gone in and shut the door, I have felt I could slay little Peter, because he had the better place, and because he looked at me through his curls, as he was carried away, as if to say: 'You are out of it!' Yet I knew I had all I deserved; and Michael's kindness and goodness and patience were beyond words. Only—only—ah, can you understand? I would sooner he had found fault and scolded; I would sooner have been shaken and called a fool, than smiled at, and left alone. I was in the nursery when he married me; I have been in the school-room ever since, trying to learn life's lessons, alone, without a teacher. Nothing has helped me to grow up. Michael has always told me I am perfect, and everything I do is perfect, and he does not want me different. But I have never really shared his life and interests. If I make idiotic mistakes he does not correct me. I have to find them out, when I repeat them before others. When I made that silly blunder about the brazen serpent, you so kindly put me right. Michael would have smiled and let it pass as not worth correcting; then I should have repeated it before a roomful of people, and wondered why they looked amused! Ah, but what do I care for people, or the world! It is my true place beside Michael I want to win. I want to 'grow up unto him in all things.' Yes, I know that is a text. I am famous for misquotations, or rather, misapplications. But it expresses my meaning—as the duchess remarks, when she has said something mild under provocation, and her parrot swears!— And now tell me, dear wise kind doctor; you, who have been the lifelong friend of that grand creature, Jane Dalmain; you, who have done so much for dozens of women I know; tell me how I can cease to be inadequate towards my husband."

The passionate flow of words ceased suddenly. Lady Ingleby leaned back against the cushions.

Peter sighed in his sleep.

A clock in the hall chimed the quarter after six.

The doctor looked steadily into the fire. He seemed to find speech difficult.

At last he said, in a voice which shook slightly: "Dear Lady Ingleby, he did not—he does not—think you so."

"No, no!" she cried, sitting forward again. "He thinks of me nothing but what is kind and right. But he never expected me to be more than a nice, affectionate, good-looking dog; and I—I have not known how to be better than his expectations. But, although he is so patient, he sometimes grows unutterably tired of being with me. All other pet creatures are dumb; but I love talking, and I constantly say silly things, which do not sound silly, until I have said them. He goes off to Norway, fishing; to the Engadine, mountain-climbing; to this horrid war, risking his precious life. Anywhere to get away alone; anywhere to——"

"Hush," said the doctor, and laid a firm brown hand, for a moment, on the white fluttering fingers. "You are overwrought by the suspense of these past weeks. You know perfectly well that Lord Ingleby volunteered for this border war because he was so keen on experimenting with his new explosives, and on trying these ideas for using electricity in modern warfare, at which he has worked so long."

"Oh, yes, I know," said Myra, smiling wistfully. "Tiresome things, which keep him hours in his laboratory. And he has some very clever plan for long distance signalling from fort to fort—hieroglyphics in the sky, isn't it? you know what I mean. But the fact that he volunteered into all this danger, merely to do experimenting, makes it harder to bear than if he had been at the head of his old regiment, and gone at the imperative call of duty. However—nothing matters so long as he comes home safely. And now you—you, Sir Deryck—must help me to become a real helpmeet to Michael. Tell me how you helped—oh, very well, we will not mention names. But give me wise advice. Give me hope; give me courage. Make me strong."

The doctor looked at the clock; and, even as he looked, the chimes in the hall rang out the half-hour.

"You have not yet told me," he said, speaking very slowly, as if listening for some other sound; "you have not yet told me, your second reason for leaving town."

"Ah," said Lady Ingleby, and her voice held a deeper, older, tone—a note bordering on tragedy. "Ah! I left town, Sir Deryck, because other people were teaching me love-lessons, and I did not want to learn them apart from Michael. I stayed with Jane Dalmain

15

and her blind husband, before they went back to Gleneesh. You remember? They were in town for the production of his symphony. I saw that ideal wedded life, and I realised something of what a perfect mating of souls could mean. And then—well, there were others; people who did not understand how wholly I am Michael's; nothing actually wrong; but not so fresh and youthful as Billy's innocent adoration; and I feared I should accidentally learn what only Michael must teach. Therefore I fled away! Oh, doctor; if I ever learned from another man, that which I have failed to learn from my own husband, I should lie at Michael's feet and implore him to kill me!"

The doctor looked up at the portrait over the mantelpiece. The calm passionless face smiled blandly at the tiny dog. One sensitive hand, white and delicate as a woman's, was raised, forefinger uplifted, gently holding the attention of the little animal's eager eyes. The magic skill of the artist supplied the doctor with the key to the problem. A woman—as mate, as wife, as part of himself, was not a necessity in the life of this thinker, inventor, scholar, saint. He could appreciate dumb devotion; he was capable of unlimited kindness, leniency, patience, toleration. But woman and dog alike, remained outside the citadel of his inner self. Had not her eyes resembled those of a favourite spaniel, he would very probably not have wedded the lovely woman who, now, during ten years had borne his name; and even then he might not have done so, had not the tyranny of her mother, awakening his instinct of protection towards the weak and oppressed, aroused in him a determination to withstand that tyranny, and to carry her off triumphantly to freedom.

The longer the doctor looked, the more persistently the picture said; "We two; and where does she come in?"—Righteous wrath arose in the heart of Deryck Brand; for his ideal as to man's worship of woman was a high one. As he thought of the closed door; of the lonely wife, humbly jealous of a toy-poodle, yet blaming herself only, for her loneliness, his jaw set, and his brow darkened. And all the while he listened for a sound from the outer world which must soon come.

Lady Ingleby noticed his intent gaze, and, leaning forward, also looked up at the picture. The firelight shone on her lovely face, and on the gleaming softness of her hair. Her lips parted in a tender smile; a pure radiance shone from her eyes.

"Ah, he is so good!" she said. "In all the years, he has never once spoken harshly to me. And see how lovingly he looks at Peter, who really is a most unattractive little dog. Did you ever hear the duchess's bon mot about Michael? He and I once stayed together at

16

Overdene; but she did not ask us again until he was abroad, fishing in Norway; so of course I went by myself. The duchess always does those things frankly, and explains them. Therefore on this occasion she said: 'My dear, I enjoy a visit from you; but you must only come, when you can come alone. I will never undertake again, to live up to your good Michael. It really was a case of St. Michael and All Angels. He was St. Michael, and we had to be all angels!' Wasn't it like the duchess; and a beautiful testimony to Michael's consistent goodness? Oh, I wish you knew him better. And, for the matter of that, I wish I knew him better! But after all I am his wife. Nothing can rob me of that. And don't you think—when Michael comes home this time—somehow, all will be different; better than ever before?"

The hall clock chimed three-quarters after the hour.

The clang of a bell resounded through the silent house.

Peter sat up, and barked once, sharply.

The doctor rose and stood with his back to the fire, facing the door.

Myra's question remained unanswered.

Hurried steps approached.

A footman entered, with a telegram for Lady Ingleby.

She took it with calm fingers, and without the usual sinking of the heart from sudden apprehension. Her mind was full of the conversation of the moment, and the doctor's presence made her feel so strong and safe; so sure of no approach of evil tidings.

She did not hear Sir Deryck's quiet voice say to the man: "You need not wait."

As the door closed, the doctor turned away, and stood looking into the fire.

The room was very still.

Lady Ingleby opened her telegram, unfolded it slowly, and read it through twice.

Afterwards she sat on, in such absolute silence that, at length, the doctor turned and looked at her.

She met his eyes, quietly.

"Sir Deryck," she said, "it is from the War Office. They tell me Michael has been killed. Do you think it is true?"

She handed him the telegram. Taking it from her, he read it in silence. Then: "Dear Lady Ingleby," he said, very gently, "I fear there is no doubt. He has given his life for his country. You will be as brave in giving him, as he would wish his wife to be."

Myra smiled; but the doctor saw her face slowly whiten.

"Yes," she said; "oh, yes! I will not fail him. I will be

17

adequate—at last." Then, as if a sudden thought had struck her: "Did you know of this? Is it why you came?"

"Yes," said the doctor, slowly. "The duchess sent me. She was at the War Office this morning when the news came in, inquiring for Ronald Ingram, who has been wounded, and is down with fever. She telephoned for me, and insisted on the telegram being kept back until six o'clock this evening, in order to give me time to get here, and to break the news to you first, if it seemed well."

Myra gazed at him, wide-eyed. "And you let me say all that, about Michael and myself?"

"Dear lady," said the doctor, and few had ever heard that deep firm voice, so nearly tremulous, "I could not stop you. But you did not say one word which was not absolutely loving and loyal."

"How could I have?" queried Myra, her face growing whiter, and her eyes wider and more bright. "I have never had a thought which was not loyal and loving."

"I know," said the doctor. "Poor brave heart,—I know."

Myra took up the telegram, and read it again.

"Killed," she said; "killed. I wish I knew how."

"The duchess is ready to come to you immediately, if you would like to have her," suggested the doctor.

"No," said Myra, smiling vaguely. "No; I think not. Not unless dear mamma comes. If that happens we must wire for the duchess, because now—now Michael is away—she is the only person who can cope with mamma. But please not, otherwise; because—well, you see,—she said she could not live up to Michael; and it does not sound funny now."

"Is there anybody you would wish sent for at once?" inquired the doctor, wondering how much larger and brighter those big grey eyes could grow; and whether any living face had ever been so absolutely colourless.

"Anybody I should wish sent for at once? I don't know. Oh, yes—there is one person; if she could come. Jane—you know? Jane Dalmain. I always say she is like the bass of a tune; so solid, and satisfactory, and beneath one. Nothing very bad could happen, if Jane were there. But of course this has happened; hasn't it?"

The doctor sat down.

"I wired to Gleneesh this morning," he said. "Jane will be here early to-morrow."

"Then lots of people knew before I did?" said Lady Ingleby.

The doctor did not answer.

She rose, and stood looking down into the fire; her tall graceful figure drawn up to its full height, her back to the doctor, whose watchful eyes never left her for an instant.

18

Suddenly she looked across to Lord Ingleby's chair.

"And I believe Peter knew," she said, in a loud, high-pitched voice. "Good heavens! Peter knew; and refused his food because Michael was dead. And I said he had dyspepsia! Michael, oh Michael! Your wife didn't know you were dead; but your dog knew! Oh Michael, Michael! Little Peter knew!"

She lifted her arms toward the picture of the big man and the tiny dog.

Then she swayed backward.

The doctor caught her, as she fell.

CHAPTER IV

IN SAFE HANDS

All through the night Lady Ingleby lay gazing before her, with bright unseeing eyes.

The quiet woman from the Lodge, who had been, before her own marriage, a devoted maid-companion to Lady Ingleby, arrived in speechless sorrow, and helped the doctor tenderly with all there was to do.

But when consciousness returned, and realisation, they were accompanied by no natural expressions of grief; simply a settled stony silence; the white set face; the bright unseeing eyes.

Margaret O'Mara knelt, and wept, and prayed, kissing the folded hands upon the silken quilt. But Lady Ingleby merely smiled vaguely; and once she said: "Hush, my dear Maggie. At last we will be adequate."

Several times during the night the doctor came, sitting silently beside the bed, with watchful eyes and quiet touch. Myra scarcely noticed him, and again he wondered how much larger the big grey eyes would grow, in the pale setting of that lovely face.

Once he signed to the other watcher to follow him into the corridor. Closing the door, he turned and faced her. He liked this quiet woman, in her simple black merino gown, linen collar and cuffs, and neatly braided hair. There was an air of refinement and gentle self-control about her, which pleased the doctor.

"Mrs. O'Mara," he said; "she must weep, and she must sleep."

"She does not weep easily, sir," replied Margaret O'Mara, "and I have known her to lie widely awake throughout an entire night with less cause for sorrow than this."

"Ah," said the doctor; and he looked keenly at the woman from the Lodge. "I wonder what else you have known?" he thought. But he did not voice the conjecture. Deryck Brand rarely asked questions of a third person. His patients never had to find out that his knowledge of them came through the gossip or the breach of confidence of others.

At last he could allow that fixed unseeing gaze no longer. He decided to do what was necessary, with a quiet nod, in response to Margaret O'Mara's imploring look. He turned back the loose sleeve of the silk nightdress, one firm hand grasped the soft arm beneath it; the other passed over it for a moment with swift skilful pressure. Even Margaret's anxious eyes saw nothing more; and afterwards

Myra often wondered what could have caused that tiny scar upon the whiteness of her arm.

Before long she was quietly asleep. The doctor stood looking down upon her. There was tragedy to him in this perfect loveliness. Now the clear candour of the grey eyes was veiled, the childlike look was no longer there. It was the face of a woman—and of a woman who had lived, and who had suffered.

Watching it, the doctor reviewed the history of those ten years of wedded life; piecing together that which she herself had told him; his own shrewd surmisings; and facts, which were common knowledge.

So much for the past. The present, for a few hours at least, was merciful oblivion. What would the future bring? She had bravely and faithfully put from her all temptation to learn the glory of life, and the completeness of love, from any save from her own husband. And he had failed to teach. Can the deaf teach harmony, or the blind reveal the beauties of blended colour?

But the future held no such limitations. The "garden enclosed" was no longer barred against all others by an owner who ignored its fragrance. The gate would be on the latch, though all unconscious until an eager hand pressed it, that its bolts and bars were gone, and it dare swing open wide.

"Ah," mused the doctor. "Will the right man pass by? Youth teaches youth; but is there a man amongst us strong enough, and true enough, and pure enough, to teach this woman, nearing thirty, lessons which should have been learned during the golden days of girlhood. Surely somewhere on this earth the One Man walks, and works, and waits, to whom she is to be the One Woman? God send him her way, in the fulness of time."

And in that very hour—while at last Myra slept, and the doctor watched, and mused, and wondered—in that very hour, under an Eastern sky, a strong man, sick of life, worn and disillusioned, fighting a deadly fever, in the sultry atmosphere of a soldier's tent, cried out in bitterness of soul: "O God, let me die!" Then added the "never-the-less" which always qualifies a brave soul's prayer for immunity from pain: "Unless—unless, O God, there be still some work left on this earth which only I can do."

And the doctor had just said: "Send him her way, O God, in the fulness of time."

The two prayers reached the Throne of Omniscience together.

Deryck Brand, looking up, saw the quiet eyes of Margaret O'Mara gazing gratefully at him, across the bed. "Thank you," she whispered.

He smiled. "Never to be done lightly, Mrs. O'Mara," he said.

21

"Everything else should be tried first. But there are exceptions to the strictest rules, and it is fatal weakness to hesitate when confronted by the exception. Send for me, when she wakes; and, meanwhile, lie down on that couch yourself and have some sleep. You are worn out."

The doctor turned away; but not before he had caught the sudden look of dumb anguish which leaped into those quiet eyes. He reached the door; paused a moment; then came back.

"Mrs. O'Mara," he said, with a hand upon her shoulder, "you have a sorrow of your own?"

She drew away from him, in terror. "Oh, hush!" she whispered. "Don't ask! Don't unnerve me, sir. Help me to think of her, only." Then, more calmly: "But of course I shall think of none but her, while she needs me. Only—only, sir—as you are so kind—" she drew from her bosom a crumpled telegram, and handed it to the doctor. "Mine came at the same time as hers," she said, simply.

The doctor unfolded the War Office message.

Regret to report Sergeant O'Mara killed in assault on Targai yesterday.

"He was a good husband," said Margaret O'Mara, simply; "and we were very happy."

The doctor held out his hand. "I am proud to have met you, Mrs. O'Mara. This seems to me the bravest thing I have ever known a woman do."

She smiled through her tears. "Thank you, sir," she said, tremulously. "But it is easier to bear my own sorrow, when I have work to do for her."

"God Himself comfort you, my friend," said Deryck Brand, and it was all he could trust his voice to say; nor was he ashamed that he had to fumble blindly for the handle of the door.

The doctor had finished breakfast, and was asking Groatley for a time-table, when word reached him that Lady Ingleby was awake. He went upstairs immediately.

Myra was sitting up in bed, propped with pillows. Her cheeks were flushed; her eyes bright and hard.

She held out her hand to the doctor.

"How good you have been," she said, speaking very fast, in a high unnatural voice: "I am afraid I have given you a great deal of trouble. I don't remember much about last night, excepting that they said Michael had been killed. Has Michael really been killed, do you think? And will they give me details? Surely I have a right to know details. Nothing can alter the fact that I was Michael's wife,

22

can it? Do go to breakfast, Maggie. There is nothing gained by standing there, smiling, and saying you do not want any breakfast. Everybody wants breakfast at nine o'clock in the morning. I should want breakfast, if Michael had not been killed. Tell her she ought to have breakfast, Sir Deryck. I believe she has been up all night. It is such a comfort to have her. She is so brave and bright; and so full of sympathy."

"She is very brave," said the doctor; "and you are right as to her need of breakfast. Go down-stairs for a little while, Mrs. O'Mara. I will stay with Lady Ingleby."

She moved obediently to the door; but Sir Deryck reached it before her. And the famous London specialist held the door open for the sergeant's young widow, with an air of deference such as he would hardly have bestowed upon a queen.

Then he came back to Lady Ingleby. His train left in three-quarters of an hour. But his task here was not finished. She had slept; but before he dare leave her, she must weep.

"Where is Peter?" inquired the excited voice from the bed. "He always barks to be let out, in the morning; but I have heard nothing of him yet."

"He was exhausted last night, poor little chap," said the doctor. "He could scarcely walk. I carried him up, myself; and put him on the bed in the next room. The coat was still there, I wrapped him in it. He licked my hand, and lay down, content."

"I want to see him," said Lady Ingleby. "Michael loved him. He seems all I have left of Michael."

"I will fetch him," said the doctor.

He went into the adjoining room, leaving the door ajar. Myra heard him reach the bed. Then followed a long silence.

"What is it?" she called at last. "Is he not there? Why are you so long?"

Then the doctor came back. He carried something in his arms, wrapped in the old shooting jacket.

"Dear Lady Ingleby," he said, "little Peter is dead. He must have died during the night, in his sleep. He was lying just as I left him, curled up in the coat; but he is quite cold and stiff. Faithful little heart!" said the doctor, with emotion, holding his burden, tenderly.

"What!" cried Myra, with both arms outstretched. "Peter has died, because Michael is dead; and I—I have not even shed a tear!" She fell back among the pillows in a paroxysm of weeping.

The doctor stood by, silently; uncertain what to do. Myra's sobs grew more violent, shaking the bed with their convulsive force.

23

Then she began to shriek inarticulately about Michael and Peter, and to sob again, with renewed violence.

At that moment the doctor heard the horn of a motor-car in the avenue; then, almost immediately, the clang of the bell, and the sounds of an arrival below. A look of immense relief came into his face. He went to the top of the great staircase, and looked over.

The Honourable Mrs. Dalmain had arrived. The doctor saw her tall figure, in a dark green travelling coat, walk rapidly across the hall.

"Jane!" he said. "Jeanette! Ah, I knew you would not fail us! Come straight up. You have arrived at the right moment."

Jane looked up, and saw the doctor standing at the top of the stairs; something wrapped in an old coat, held carefully in his arms. She threw him one smile of greeting and assurance; then, wasting no time in words, rapidly pulled off her coat, hat, and fur gloves, flinging them in quick succession to the astonished butler. The doctor only waited to see her actually mounting the stairs. Then, passing through Lady Ingleby's room, he laid Peter's little body back on his dead master's bed, still wrapped in the old tweed coat.

As he stepped back into Lady Ingleby's room, closing the door between, he saw Jane Dalmain kneel down beside the bed, and gather the weeping form into her arms, with a gesture of immense protective tenderness.

"Oh Jane," sobbed Lady Ingleby, as she hid her face in the sweet comfort of that generous bosom; "Oh Jane! Michael has been killed! And little Peter died, because Michael was dead. Little Peter died, and I had not even shed a tear!"

The doctor passed quickly out, closing the door behind him. He did not wait to hear the answer. He knew it would be wise, and kind, and right. He left his patient in safe hands. Jane was there, at last. All would be well.

24

CHAPTER V

LADY INGLEBY'S REST-CURE

From the moment when the express for Cornwall had slowly but irrevocably commenced to glide away from the Paddington platform; when she had looked her last upon Margaret O'Mara's anxious devoted face, softly framed in her simple widow's bonnet; when she had realised that her somewhat original rest-cure had really safely commenced, and that she was leaving, not only her worries, but her very identity behind her—Lady Ingleby had leaned back with closed eyes in a corner of her reserved compartment, and given herself up to quiet retrospection.

The face, in repose, was sad—a quiet sadness, as of regret which held no bitterness. The cheek, upon which the dark fringe of lashes rested, was white and thin having lost the tint and contour of perfect health. But, every now and then, during those hours of retrospection, the wistful droop of the sweet expressive mouth curved into a smile, and a dimple peeped out unexpectedly, giving a look of youthfulness to the tired face.

When London and, its suburbs were completely left behind, and the summer sunshine blazed through the window from the clear blue of a radiant June sky, Lady Ingleby leaned forward, watching the rapid unfolding of country lanes and hedges; wide commons, golden with gorse; fir woods, carpeted with blue-bells; mossy banks, overhung with wild roses, honeysuckle, and traveller's-joy; the indescribable greenness and soft fragrance of England in early summer; and, as she watched, a responsive light shone in her sweet grey eyes. The drear sadness of autumn, the deadness of winter, the chill uncertainty of spring—all these were over and gone. "Flowers appear on the earth; the time of the singing of birds is come," murmurs the lover of Canticles; and in Myra Ingleby's sad heart there blossomed timidly, flowers of hope; vague promise of future joy, which life might yet hold in store. A blackbird in the hawthorn, trilled gaily; and Myra softly sang, to an air of Garth Dalmain's, the "Blackbird's Song."

> "Wake, wake,
> Sad heart!
> Rise up, and sing!
> On God's fair earth, 'mid blossoms blue.
> Fresh hope must ever spring.

There is no room for sad despair,
When heaven's love is everywhere."

Then, as the train sped onward through Wiltshire, Somerset, and Devon, Lady Ingleby felt the mantle of her despondence slipping from her, and reviewed the past, much as a prisoner might glance back into his dark narrow cell, from the sunlight of the open door, as he stood at last on the threshold of liberty.

Seven months had gone by since, on that chill November evening, the news of Lord Ingleby's death had reached Shenstone. The happenings of the weeks which followed, now seemed vague and dreamlike to Myra, just a few events standing out clearly from the dim blur of misery. She remembered the reliable strength of the doctor; the unselfish devotion of Margaret O'Mara; the unspeakable comfort of Jane's wholesome understanding tenderness. Then the dreaded arrival of her mother; followed, immediately, according to promise, by the protective advent of Georgina, Duchess of Meldrum; after which, tragedy and comedy walked hand in hand; and the silence of mourning was enlivened by the "Hoity-toity!" of the duchess, and the indignant sniffs of Mrs. Coller-Cray.

Later on, details of Lord Ingleby's death came to hand, and his widow had to learn that he had fallen—at the attempt upon Targai, it is true—but the victim of an accident; losing his life, not at the hands of the savage enemy, but through the unfortunate blunder of a comrade. Myra never very clearly grasped the details:—a wall to be undermined; his own patent and fearful explosive; the grim enthusiasm with which he insisted upon   placing it himself, arranging to have it fired by his patent electrical plan. Then the mistaking of a signal; the fatal pressing of a button five minutes too soon; an electric flash in the mine, a terrific explosion, and instant death to the man whose skill and courage had made the gap through which crowds of cheering British soldiers, bursting from the silent darkness, dashed to expectant victory.

When full details reached the War Office, a Very Great Personage called at her house in Park Lane personally to explain to Lady Ingleby the necessity for the hushing up of some of these greatly-to-be-deplored facts. The whole unfortunate occurrence had largely partaken of the nature of an experiment. The explosive, the new method of signalling, the portable electric plant—all these were being used by Lord Ingleby and the young officers who assisted him, more or less experimentally and unofficially. The man whose unfortunate mistake caused the accident had an important career before him. His name must not be allowed to transpire. It would be unfair that a future of great promise should be blighted by what was

26

an obvious accident. The few to whom the name was known had been immediately pledged to secrecy. Of course it would be confidentially given to Lady Ingleby if she really desired to hear it, but——

Then Myra took a very characteristic line. She sat up with instant decision; her pale face flushed, and her large pathetic grey eyes shone with sudden brightness.

"Pardon me, sir," she said, "for interposing; but I never wish to know that name. My husband would have been the first to desire that it should not be told. And, personally, I should be sorry that there should be any man on earth whose hand I could not bring myself to touch in friendship. The hand that widowed me, did so without intention. Let it remain always to me an abstract instrument of the will of Providence. I shall never even try to guess to which of Michael's comrades that hand belonged."

Lady Ingleby was honest in making this decision; and the Very Great Personage stepped into his brougham, five minutes later, greatly relieved, and filled with admiration for Lord Ingleby's beautiful and right-minded widow. She had always been all that was most charming. Now she added sound good sense, to personal charm. Excellent! Incomparable! Poor Ingleby! Poor—Ah! he must not be mentioned, even in thought.

Yes; Lady Ingleby was absolutely honest in coming to her decision. And yet, from that moment, two names revolved perpetually in her mind, around a ceaseless question—the only men mentioned constantly by Michael in his letters as being always with him in his experiments, sharing his interests and his dangers: Ronald Ingram, and Billy Cathcart—dear boys, both; her devoted adorers; almost her dearest, closest friends; faithful, trusted, tried. And now the haunting question circled around all thought of them: "Was it Ronald? Or was it Billy? Which? Billy or Ronnie? Ronnie or Billy?" Myra had said: "I shall never even try to guess," and she had said it honestly. She did not try to guess. She guessed, in spite of trying not to do so; and the certainty, and yet uncertainty of her surmisings told on her nerves, becoming a cause of mental torment which was with her, subconsciously, night and day.

Time went on. The frontier war was over. England, as ever, had been bound to win in the end; and England had won. It had merely been a case of time; of learning wisdom by a series of initial mistakes; of expending a large amount of British gold and British blood. England's supremacy was satisfactorily asserted; and, those of her brave troops who had survived the initial mistakes, came home; among them Ronald Ingram and Billy Cathcart; the former obviously older than when he went away, gaunt and worn, pale

27

beneath his bronze, showing unmistakable signs of the effects of a severe wound and subsequent fever. "Too interesting for words," said the Duchess of Meldrum to Lady Ingleby, recounting her first sight of him. "If only I were fifty years younger than I am, I would marry the dear boy immediately, take him down to Overdene, and nurse him back to health and strength. Oh, you need not look incredulous, my dear Myra! I always mean what I say, as you very well know."

But Lady Ingleby denied all suspicion of incredulity, and merely suggested languidly, that—bar the matrimonial suggestion—the programme was an excellent one, and might well be carried out. Young Ronald being of the same opinion, he was soon installed at Overdene, and had what he afterwards described as the time of his life, being pampered, spoiled, and petted by the dear old duchess, and never allowing her to suspect that one of the chief attractions of Overdene lay in the fact that it was within easy motoring distance of Shenstone Park.

Billy returned as young, as inconsequent, as irrepressible as ever. And yet in him also, Myra was conscious of a subtle change, for which she, all too readily, found a reason, far removed from the real one.

The fact was this. Both young men, in their romantic devotion to her, had yet been true to their own manhood, and loyal, at heart, to Lord Ingleby. But their loyalty had always been with effort. Therefore, when—the strain relaxed—they met her again, they were intensely conscious of her freedom and of their own resultant liberty. This produced in them, when with her, a restraint and shyness which Myra naturally construed into a confirmation of her own suspicions. She, having never found it the smallest effort to remember she was Michael's, and to be faithful in every thought to him, was quite unconscious of her liberty. There having been no strain in remaining true to the instincts of her own pure, honest, honourable nature, there was no tension to relax.

So it very naturally came to pass that when one day Ronald Ingram had sat long with her, silently studying his boots, his strong face tense and miserable, every now and then looking furtively at her, then, as his eyes met the calm friendliness of hers, dropping them again to the floor:—"Poor Ronnie," she mused, "with his 'important career' before him. Undoubtedly it was he who did it. And Billy knows it. See how fidgety Billy is, while Ronnie sits with me."

But by-and-by it would be: "No; of course it was Billy—dear hot-headed impulsive young Billy; and Ronald, knowing it, feels guilty also. Poor little Billy, who was as a son to Michael! There was

28

no mistaking the emotion in his face just now, when I merely laid my hand on his. Oh, impetuous scatter-brained boy!... Dear heavens! I wish he wouldn't hand me the bread-and-butter."

Then, into this atmosphere of misunderstanding and uncertainty, intruded a fresh element. A first-cousin of Lord Ingleby's, to whom had come the title, minus the estates, came to the conclusion that title and estates might as well go together. To that end, intruding upon her privacy on every possible occasion, he proceeded to pay business-like court to Lady Ingleby.

Thus rudely Myra awoke to the understanding of her liberty. At once, her whole outlook on life was changed. All things bore a new significance. Ronnie and Billy ceased to be comforts. Ronnie's nervous misery assumed a new importance; and, coupled with her own suspicions, filled her with a dismayed horror. The duchess's veiled jokes took point, and hurt. A sense of unprotected loneliness engulfed her. Every man became a prospective and dreaded suitor; every woman's remarks seemed to hold an innuendo. Her name in the papers distracted her.

She recognised the morbidness of her condition, even while she felt unable to cope with it; and, leaving Shenstone suddenly, came up to town, and consulted Sir Deryck Brand.

"Oh, my friend," she said, "help me! I shall never face life again."

The doctor heard her patiently, aiding the recital by his strong understanding silence.

Then he said, quietly: "Dear lady, the diagnosis is not difficult. Also there is but one possible remedy." He paused.

Lady Ingleby's imploring eyes and tense expectancy, besought his verdict.

"A rest-cure," said the doctor, with finality.

"Horrors, no!" cried Myra; "Would you shut me up within four walls; cram me with rice pudding and every form of food I most detest; send a dreadful woman to pound, roll, and pommel me, and tell me gruesome stories; keep out all my friends, all letters, all books, all news; and, after six weeks send me out into the world again, with my figure gone, and not a sane thought upon any subject under the sun? Dear doctor, think of it! Stout, and an idiot! Oh, give me something in a bottle, to shake, and take three times a day—and let me go!"

The doctor smiled. He was famed for his calm patience.

"Your somewhat highly coloured description, dear Lady Ingleby, applies to a form of rest-cure such as I rarely, if ever, recommend. In your case it would be worse than useless. We should gain nothing by shutting you up with the one person who is doing you harm, and from whom we must contrive your escape."

"The one person—?" queried Myra, wide-eyed.

"A charming person," smiled the doctor, "where the rest of mankind are concerned; but very bad for you just now."

"But—whom?" questioned Myra, again. "Whom can you mean?"

"I mean Lady Ingleby," replied the doctor, gravely. "When I send you away for your rest-cure, Lady Ingleby with her worries and questionings, doubts and fears, must be left behind. I shall send you to a little out-of-the-world village on the wild sea coast of Cornwall, where you know nobody, and nobody knows you. You must go incognito, as 'Miss' or 'Mrs.'—anything you please. Your rest-cure will consist primarily in being set free, for a time, from Lady Ingleby's position, predicament, and perplexities. You must send word to all intimate friends, telling them you are going into retreat, and they must not write until they hear again. You will have leave to write one letter a week, to one person only; and that person must be one of whom I can approve. You must eat plenty of wholesome food; roam about all day long in the open-air; rise early, retire early; live entirely in a simple, beautiful, wholesome present, firmly avoiding all remembrance of a sad past, and all anticipation of an uncertain future. Nobody is to know where you are, excepting myself, and the one friend to whom you may write. But we will arrange that somebody—say, for instance, your devoted attendant from the Lodge, shall hold herself free to come to you at an hour's notice, should you be overwhelmed with a sudden sense of loneliness. The knowledge of this, will probably keep the need from arising. You can communicate with me daily if you like, by letter or by telegram; but other people must not know where you are. I do not wish you followed by the anxious or restless thoughts of many minds. To-morrow I will give you the name of a place I recommend, and of a comfortable hotel where you can order rooms. It must be a place you have never seen, probably one of which you have never heard. We are nearing the end of May. I should like you to start on the first of June. If you want a house-party at Shenstone this summer, you may invite your guests for the first of July. Lady Ingleby will be at home again by then, fully able to maintain her reputation as a hostess of unequalled charm, graciousness, and popularity. Morbid self-consciousness is a condition of mind from which you have hitherto been so completely free, that this unexpected attack has altogether unnerved you, and requires prompt and uncompromising measures.... Yes, Jane Dalmain may be your correspondent. You could not have chosen better."

This was the doctor's verdict and prescription; and, as his patients never disputed the one, or declined to take the other, Myra found herself, on "the glorious first of June" flying south in the Great Western express, bound for the little fishing village of Tregarth where she had ordered rooms at the Moorhead Inn, in the name of Mrs. O'Mara.

CHAPTER VI

AT THE MOORHEAD INN

The ruddy glow of a crimson sunset illumined cliff and hamlet, tinting the distant ocean into every shade of golden glory, as Myra walked up the gravelled path to the rustic porch of the Moorhead Inn, and looked around her with a growing sense of excited refreshment.

She had come on foot from the little wayside station, her luggage following in a barrow; and this mode of progression, minus a footman and maid, and carrying her own cloak, umbrella, and travelling-bag, was in itself a charming novelty.

At the door, she was received by the proprietress, a stately lady in black satin, wearing a double row of large jet beads, who reminded her instantly of all Lord Ingleby's maiden aunts. She seemed an accentuated, dignified, concentrated embodiment of them all; and Myra longed for Billy, to share the joke.

"Aunt Ingleby" requested Mrs. O'Mara to walk in, and hoped she had had a pleasant journey. Then she rang a very loud bell twice, in order to summon a maid to show her to her room; and, the maid not appearing at once, requested Mrs. O'Mara meanwhile to write her name in the visitors' book.

Lady Ingleby walked into the hall, passing a smoking-room on the left, and, noting a door, with "Coffee Room" upon it in gold lettering, down a short passage immediately opposite. Up from the centre of the hall, on her right, went the rather wide old-fashioned staircase; and opposite to it, against the wall, between the smoking-room and a door labelled "Reception Room," stood a marble-topped table. Lying open upon this table was a ponderous visitors' book. A fresh page had been recently commenced, as yet only containing four names. The first three were dated May the th, and read, in crabbed precise writing:

Miss Amelia Murgatroyd, Miss Eliza Murgatroyd,
Miss Susannah Murgatroyd ..... Lawn View, Putney.

Below these, bearing date a week later, in small precise writing of unmistakable character and clearness, the name:

Jim Airth ..... London.

Pen and ink lay ready, and, without troubling to remove her glove, Lady Ingleby wrote beneath, in large, somewhat sprawling, handwriting:

Mrs. O'Mara ..... The Lodge, Shenstone.

A maid appeared, took her cloak and bag, and preceded her up the stairs.

As she reached the turn of the staircase, Lady Ingleby paused, and looked back into the hall.

The door of the smoking-room opened, and a very tall man came out, taking a pipe from the pocket of his loose Norfolk jacket. As he strolled into the hall, his face reminded her of Ronnie's, deep-bronzed and thin; only it was an older face—strong, rugged, purposeful. The heavy brown moustache could not hide the massive cut of chin and jaw.

Catching sight of a fresh name in the book, he paused; then laying one large hand upon the table, bent over and read it.

Myra stood still and watched, noting the broad shoulders, and the immense length of limb in the leather leggings.

He appeared to study the open page longer than was necessary for the mere reading of the name. Then, without looking round, reached up, took a cap from the antler of a stag's head high up on the wall, stuck it on the back of his head; swung round, and went out through the porch, whistling like a blackbird.

"Jim Airth," said Myra to herself, as she moved slowly on; "Jim Airth of London. What an address! He might just as well have put: 'of the world!' A cross between a guardsman and a cowboy; and very likely he will turn out to be a commercial-traveller." Then, as she reached the landing and came in sight of the rosy-cheeked maid, holding open the door of a large airy bedroom, she added with a whimsical smile: "All the same, I wish I had taken the trouble to write more neatly."

CHAPTER VII

MRS. O'MARA'S CORRESPONDENCE

Letter from Lady Ingleby to the Honourable Mrs. Dalmain.

The Moorhead Inn,
Tregarth, Cornwall.

My dear Jane,

Having been here a week, I think it is time I commenced my first letter to you.

How does it feel to be a person considered pre-eminently suitable to minister to a mind diseased? Doesn't it give you a sense of being, as it were, rice pudding, or Brand's essence, or Maltine; something essentially safe and wholesome? You should have heard how Sir Deryck jumped at you, as soon as your name was mentioned, tentatively, as my possible correspondent. I had barely whispered it, when he leapt, and clinched the matter. I believe "wholesome" was an adjective mentioned. I hope you do not mind, dear Jane. I must confess, I would sooner be macaroons or oyster-patties, even at the risk of giving my friends occasional indigestion. But then I have never gone in for the rôle of being helpful, in which you excel. Not that it is a "rôle" with you, dear Jane. Rather, it is an essential characteristic. You walk in, and find a hopeless tangle; gather up the threads in those firm capable hands; deftly sort and hold them; and, lo, the tangle is over; the skein of life is once more ready for winding!

Well, there is not much tangle about me just now, thanks to our dear doctor's most excellent prescription. It was a veritable stroke of genius, this setting me free from myself. From the first day, the sense of emancipation was indescribable. I enjoy being addressed as "Ma'am"; I revel in being without a maid, though it takes me ages to do my hair, and I have serious thoughts of wearing it in pigtails down my back! When I remember the poor, harassed, exhausted, society-self I left behind, I feel like buying a wooden spade and bucket and starting out, all by myself, to build sand-castles on this delightful shore. I have no one to play with, for I am certain the Miss Murgatroyds—I am going to tell you of them—never made sand-castles; no, not even in their infancy, a century ago! They must always have been the sort of children who wore white frilled bloomers, poplin frocks, and large leghorn hats with ribbons tied beneath their excellent little chins, and walked demurely with their governess—looking shocked at other infants who whooped and ran. I feel inclined to whoop and run, now; and the Miss Murgatroyds are quite prepared to look shocked.

But oh, the freedom of being nobody, and of having nothing to think of or do! And everything I see and hear gives me joy; a lark rising from the turf, and carolling its little self up into the blue; the great Atlantic breakers, pounding upon the shore; the fisher-folk, standing at the doors of their picturesque thatched cottages. All things seem alive, with an exuberance of living, to which I have long been a stranger.

Do you know this coast, with its high moorland, its splendid cliffs; and, far below, its sand coves, and ever-moving, rolling, surging, deep green sea? Wonderful! Beautiful! Infinite!

My Inn is charming; primitive, yet comfortable. We have excellent coffee, fried fish in perfection; real nursery toast, farm butter, and home-made bread. When you supplement these with marmalade and mulberry jam, other things all cease to be necessities.

Stray travellers come and go in motors, merely lunching, or putting up for one night; but there are only four other permanent guests. These all furnish me with unceasing interest and amusement. The three Miss Murgatroyds—oh, Jane, they are so antediluvian and quaint! Three ancient sisters,—by name, Amelia, Eliza, and Susannah. Their villa at Putney rejoices in the name of "Lawn View"; so characteristic and suitable; because no view reaching beyond the limits of their own front lawn appears to these dear ladies to be worthy of regard. They never go abroad, "excepting to the Isle of Wight," because they "do not like foreigners." A party of quite charming Americans arrived just before dinner the other day, in an automobile, and kept us lively during their flying visit. They were cordial over the consommé; friendly over the fish; and quite confidential by the time we reached the third course. But, alas, these delightful cousins from the other side, were considered "foreigners" by the Miss Murgatroyds, who consequently encased themselves in the frigid armour of their own self-conscious primness; and passed the mustard, without a smile. I felt constrained, afterwards, to apologise for my country-women; but the Americans, overflowing with appreciative good-nature, explained that they had come over expressly in order to see old British relics of every kind. They asked me whether I did not think the Miss Murgatroyds might have stepped "right out of Dickens." I was fairly nonplussed, because I thought they were going to say "out of the ark"—you know how one mentally finishes a sentence as soon as it is begun?—and I simply dared not confess that I have not read Dickens! Alas, how ignorant of our own standard literature we are apt to feel when we talk with Americans, and find it completely a part of their everyday life.

But I must tell you more about the Miss Murgatroyds—Amelia, Eliza, and Susannah. When quite at peace among themselves, which is not often, they are Milly, Lizzie, and Susie; but a little rift within the lute is marked by the immediate use of their full baptismal names. Poor Susannah being the youngest—the youthful side of sixty—and inclined to be kittenish and giddy, is very rarely "Susie." Miss Murgatroyd—Amelia—is stern and unbending. She wears a cameo brooch the size of a tablespoon, and lays down the law in precise and elegant English, even when asking Susie to pass the crumpets. Miss Eliza, the second sister, is meek and unoffending. Her attitude toward Miss Amelia is one of perpetual apology. She addresses Susie as "my dear love," excepting on occasions when Susie's behaviour has put her quite outside the pale. Then she calls her, "my dear Susannah!" and sighs. I am inclined to think Miss Eliza suffers from a demonstrative nature, which has never had an outlet.

But Susie is the lively one. Susie would be a flirt, if she dared, and if any man were bold enough to flirt with her under Miss Amelia's eye. Susie is barely fifty-five, and her elder sisters regard her as a mere child, and are very ready with reproof and correction. Susie has a pink and white complexion, a soft fat little face, and plump dimpled hands; and Susie is given to vanity. Jim Airth held open the door of the coffee-room for her one day, and Susie—I should say Susannah—has been in a flutter ever since. Poor naughty Susie! Miss Murgatroyd has changed her place at meals—they have a table in the centre of the room—and made her sit with her back to Jim Airth; who has a round table, all to himself, in the window.

Now I must tell you about Jim Airth, and of a curious coincidence connected with him, which you must not repeat to the doctor, for fear he should move me on.

Let me confess at once, that I am extremely interested in Jim Airth—and it is sweet and generous of me to admit it, for Jim Airth is not in the least interested in me! He rarely vouchsafes me a word or a glance. He is a bear, and a savage; but such a fine good-looking bear; and such a splendid and interesting savage! He is quite the tallest man I ever saw; with immense limbs, lean and big-boned; yet moves with the supple grace of an Indian. He was through that campaign last year, and had a terrible turn of sunstroke and fever, during which his head was shaved. Consequently his thick brown hair is now at the stage of standing straight up all over it like a

36

bottle-brush. I know Susie longs to smooth it down; but that would be a task beyond Susie's utmost efforts. His brows are very stern and level; and his eyes, deep-set beneath them, of that gentian blue which makes one think of Alpine heights. They can flash and gleam, on occasions, and sometimes look almost purple. He wears a heavy brown moustache, and his jaw and chin are terrifying in their masterful strength. Yet he smokes an old briar pipe; whistles like a blackbird; and derives immense amusement from playing up to naughty Susie's coyness, when the cameo brooch is turned another way. I have seen his eyes twinkle with fun when Miss Susannah has purposely let fall her handkerchief, and he has reached out a long arm, picked it up, and restored it. Whereupon Susie has hastened out, in the wake of her sisters, in a blushing flutter; Miss Eliza turning to whisper: "Oh, my dear love! Oh Susannah!" I try, when these things happen, to catch Jim Airth's merry eye, and share the humour of the situation; but he stolidly sees the wall through me on all occasions, and would tread heavily on my poor handkerchief, if I took to dropping it. Miss Murgatroyd tells me that he is a confirmed hater of feminine beauty; upon which poor Miss Susannah takes a surreptitious prink into the gold-framed mirror over the reception-room mantelpiece, and says, plaintively: "Oh, do not say that, Amelia!" But Amelia does say "that"; and a good deal more!

When first I saw Jim Airth, I thought him a cross between a cowboy and a guardsman; and I think so still. But what do you suppose he turns out to be, beside? An author! And, stranger still, he is writing an important book called Modern Warfare; its Methods and Requirements, in which he is explaining and working out many of Michael's ideas and experiments. He was right through that border war, and took part in the assault on Targai. He must have known Michael, intimately.

All this information I have from Miss Murgatroyd. I sometimes sit with them in the reception-room after dinner, where they wind wool and knit—endless winding; perpetual knitting! At five minutes to ten, Miss Murgatroyd says; "Now, my dear Eliza. Now, Susannah," which is the signal for bestowing all their goods and chattels into black satin work-bags. Then, at ten o'clock precisely, Miss Murgatroyd rises, and they procession up to bed— ah, no! I beg their pardons. The Miss Murgatroyds never "go to bed." They all "retire to rest."

Jim Airth and his doings form a favourite topic of conversation. They speak of him as "Mr. Airth," which sounds so funny. He is not the sort of person one ever could call "Mister." To me, he has been "Jim Airth," ever since I saw his name, in small neat writing, in the visitors' book. I had to put mine just beneath it, and of course I wrote "Mrs. O'Mara"; then, as an address seemed expected, added: "The Lodge, Shenstone." Just after I had written this, Jim Airth came into the hall, and stood quite still studying it. I saw him, from half-way up the stairs. At first I thought he was marvelling at my shocking handwriting; but now I believe the name "Shenstone" caught his eye. No doubt he knew it to be Michael's family-seat.

Do you know, it was so strange, the other night, Miss Murgatroyd held forth in the reception-room about Michael's death. She explained that he was "the first to dash into the breach," and "fell with his face to the foe." She also added that she used to know "poor dear Lady Ingleby," intimately. This was interesting, and seemed worthy of further inquiry. It turned out that she is a distant cousin of a weird old person who used to call every year on mamma, for a subscription to some society for promoting thrift among the inhabitants of the South Sea Islands. Dear mamma used annually to jump upon this courageous old party and flatten her out; and listening to the process was, to us, a fearful joy; but annually she returned to the charge. On one of these occasions, just before my marriage, Miss Murgatroyd accompanied her. Hence her intimate knowledge of "poor dear Lady Ingleby." Also she has a friend who, quite recently, saw Lady Ingleby driving in the Park; "and, poor thing, she had sadly gone off in looks." I felt inclined to prink in the golden mirror, after the manner of Susie, and exclaim: "Oh, do not say that, Amelia!"

Isn't it queer the way in which such people as these worthy ladies, yearn to be able to say they know us; for really, when all is said and done, we are not very much worth knowing? I would rather know a cosmopolitan cowboy, such as Jim Airth, than half the titled folk on my visiting-list.

But really, Jane, I must not mention him again, or you will think I am infected with Susie's flutter. Not so, my dear! He has shown me no little courtesies; given few signs of being conscious of my presence; barely returned my morning greeting, though my lonely table is just opposite his, in the large bay-window.

But in this new phase of life, everything seems of absorbing interest, and the individuality of the few people I see, takes on an exaggerated importance. (Really that sentence might almost be Sir Deryck's!) Also, I really believe Jim Airth's peculiar fascination consists in the fact that I am conscious of his disapproval. If he thinks of me at all, it is not with admiration, nor even with liking. And this is a novel experience; for I have been spoilt by perpetual approval, and satiated by senseless and unmerited adulation.

Oh Jane! As I walk along these cliffs, and hear the Atlantic breakers pounding against their base, far down below; as I watch the sea-gulls circling around on their strong white wings; as I realise the strength, the force, the liberty, in nature; the growth and progress which accompanies life; I feel I have never really lived. Nothing has ever felt strong, either beneath me, or around me, or against me. Had I once been mastered, and held, and made to do as another willed, I should have felt love was a reality, and life would have become worth living. But I have just dawdled through the years, doing exactly as I pleased; making mistakes, and nobody troubling to set me right; failing, and nobody disappointed that I had not succeeded.

I realise now, that there is a key to life, and a key to love, which has never been placed in my hands. What it is, I know not. But if I ever learn, it will be from just such a man as Jim Airth. I have never really talked with him, yet I am so conscious of his strength and virility, that he stands to me, in the abstract, for all that is strongest in manhood, and most vital in life.

Much of the benefit of my time here, quite unconsciously to himself, comes to me from him. When he walks into the house, whistling like a blackbird; when he hangs up his cap on an antler a foot or two higher than other people could reach; when he ploughs unhesitatingly through his meals, with a book or a paper stuck up in front of him; when he dumps his big boots out into the passage, long after the quiet house has hushed into repose, and I smile, in the darkness, at the thought of how the sound will have annoyed Miss Murgatroyd, startled Miss Eliza, and made naughty Miss Susannah's heart flutter;—when all these things happen every day, I am conscious that a clearer understanding of the past, a new strength for the future, and a fresh outlook on life, come to me, simply from the fact that he is himself, and that he is here. Jim Airth may not be a saint; but he is a man!

Dear Jane, I should scarcely venture to send you this epistle, were it not for all the adjectives—"wholesome," "helpful," "understanding," etc., which so rightly apply to you. You will not misunderstand. Of that I have no fear. But do not tell the doctor more than that I am very well, in excellent spirits, and happier than I have ever been in my life.

Tell Garth I loved his last song. How often I sing to myself, as I walk in the sea breeze and sunshine, the hairbells waving round my feet:

"On God's fair earth, 'mid blossoms blue,
Fresh hope must ever spring."

39

I trust I sing it in tune; but I know I have not much ear.

And how is your little Geoffrey? Has he the beautiful shining eyes, we all remember? I have often laughed over your account of his sojourn at Overdene, and of how our dear naughty old duchess stirred him up to rebel against his nurse. You must have had your hands full when you and Garth returned from America. Oh, Jane, how different my life would have been if I had had a little son! Ah, well!

> "There is no room for sad despair,
> When heaven's love is everywhere."

Tell Garth, I love it; but I wish he wrote simpler accompaniments. That one beats me!

Yours, dear Jane,
Gratefully and affectionately,
Myra Ingleby.

Letter from the Honourable Mrs. Dalmain to Lady Ingleby.

Castle Gleneesh, N. B.

My Dear Myra,

No, I have not the smallest objection to representing rice pudding, or anything else plain and wholesome, providing I agree with you, and suffice for the need of the moment.

I am indeed glad to have so good a report. It proves Deryck right in his diagnosis and prescription. Keep to the latter faithfully, in every detail.

I am much interested in your account of your fellow-guests at the Moorhead Inn. No, I do not misunderstand your letter; nor do I credit you with any foolish sentimentality, or Susie-like flutterings. Jim Airth stands to you for an abstract thing—uncompromising manhood, in its strength and assurance; very attractive after the loneliness and sense of being cut adrift, which have been your portion lately. Only, remember—where living men and women are concerned, the safely abstract is apt suddenly to become the perilously personal; and your future happiness may be seriously involved, before you realise the danger. I confess, I fail to understand the man's avoidance of you. He sounds the sort of fellow who would be friendly and pleasant toward all women, and passionately loyal to one. Perhaps you, with your sweet loveliness— a fact, my dear, notwithstanding the observations in the Park, of Miss Amelia's crony!—may remind him of some long-closed page of

40

past history, and he may shrink from the pain of a consequent turning of memory's leaves. No doubt Miss Susannah recalls some nice old maiden-aunt, and he can afford to respond to her blandishments.

What you say of the way in which Americans know our standard authors, reminds me of a fellow-passenger on board the Baltic, on our outward voyage—a charming woman, from Hartford, Connecticut, who sat beside us at meals. She had been spending five months in Europe, travelling incessantly, and finished up with London—her first visit to our capital—expecting to be altogether too tired to enjoy it; but found it a place of such abounding interest and delight, that life went on with fresh zest, and fatigue was forgotten. "Every street," she explained, "is so familiar. We have never seen them before, and yet they are more familiar than the streets of our native cities. It is the London of Dickens and of Thackeray. We know it all. We recognise the streets as we come to them. The places are homelike to us. We have known them all our lives." I enjoyed this tribute to our English literature. But I wonder, my dear Myra, how many streets, east of Temple Bar, in our dear old London, are "homelike" to you!

Garth insists upon sending you at once a selection of his favourites from among the works of Dickens. So expect a bulky package before long. You might read them aloud to the Miss Murgatroyds, while they knit and wind wool.

Garth thoroughly enjoyed our trip to America. You know why we went? Since he lost his sight, all sounds mean so much to him. He is so boyishly eager to hear all there is to be heard in the world. Any possibility of a new sound-experience fills him with enthusiastic expectation, and away we go! He set his heart upon hearing the thunderous roar of Niagara, so off we went, by the White Star Line. His enjoyment was complete, when at last he stood close to the Horseshoe Fall, on the Canadian side, with his hand on the rail at the place where the spray showers over you, and the great rushing boom seems all around. And as we stood there together, a little bird on a twig beside us, began to sing!—Garth is putting it all into a symphony.

How true is what you say of the genial friendliness of Americans! I was thinking it over, on our homeward voyage. It seems to me, that, as a rule, they are so far less self-conscious than we. Their minds are fully at liberty to go out at once, in keenest appreciation and interest, to meet a new acquaintance. Our senseless British greeting: "How do you do?"—that everlasting question, which neither expects nor awaits an answer, can only lead to trite remarks about the weather; whereas America's "I am happy to meet you, Mrs. Dalmain," or "I am pleased to make your acquaintance, Lady Ingleby," is an open door, through which we pass at once to fuller friendliness. Too often, in the moment of introduction, the reserved British nature turns in upon itself, sensitively debating what impression it is making; nervously afraid of being too expansive; fearful of giving itself away. But, as I said, the American mind comes forth to meet us with prompt interest and appreciative expectation; and we make more friends, in that land of ready sympathies, in half an hour, than we do in half a year of our own stiff social functions. Perhaps you will put me down as biassed in my opinion. Well, they were wondrous good to Garth and me; and we depend so greatly upon people saying exactly the right thing at the right moment. When friendly looks cannot be seen, tactful words become more than ever a necessity.

Yes, little Geoff's eyes are bright and shining, and the true golden brown. In many other ways he is very like his father.

Garth sends his love, and promises you a special accompaniment to the "Blackbird's Song," such as can easily be played with one finger!

It seems so strange to address this envelope to Mrs. O'Mara. It reminds me of a time when I dropped my own identity and used another woman's name. I only wish your experiment might end as happily as mine.

Ah, Myra dearest, there is a Best for every life! Sometimes we can only reach it by a rocky path or along a thorny way; and those who fear the pain, come to it not at all. But such of us as have attained, can testify that it is worth while. From all you have told me lately, I gather the Best has not yet come your way. Keep on expecting. Do not be content with less.

We certainly must not let Deryck know that Jim Airth—what a nice name—was at Targai. He would move you on, promptly.

Report again next week; and do abide, if necessary, beneath the safe chaperonage of the cameo brooch.

Yours, in all fidelity,
Jane Dalmain.

42

CHAPTER VIII

IN HORSESHOE COVE

Lady Ingleby sat in the honeysuckle arbour, pouring her tea from a little brown earthenware teapot, and spreading substantial slices of home-made bread with the creamiest of farm butter, when the aged postman hobbled up to the garden gate of the Moorhead Inn, with a letter for Mrs. O'Mara.

For a moment she could scarcely bring herself to open an envelope bearing another name than her own. Then, smiling at her momentary hesitation, she tore it open with the keen delight of one, who, accustomed to a dozen letters a day, has passed a week without receiving any.

She read Mrs. Dalmain's letter through rapidly; and once she laughed aloud; and once a sudden colour flamed into her cheeks.

Then she laid it down, and helped herself to honey—real heather-honey, golden in the comb.

She took up her letter again, and read it carefully, weighing each word.

Then:—"Good old Jane!" she said; "that is rather neatly put: the 'safely abstract' becoming the 'perilously personal.' She has acquired the knack of terse and forceful phraseology from her long friendship with the doctor. I can do it myself, when I try; only, my Sir Derycky sentences are apt merely to sound well, and mean nothing at all. And—after all—does this of Jane's mean anything worthy of consideration? Could six foot five of abstraction—eating its breakfast in complete unconsciousness of one's presence, returning one's timid 'good-morning' with perfunctory politeness, and relegating one, while still debating the possibility of venturing a remark on the weather, to obvious oblivion—ever become perilously personal?"

Lady Ingleby laughed again, returned the letter to its envelope, and proceeded to cut herself a slice of home-made currant cake. As she finished it, with a final cup of tea, she thought with amusement of the difference between this substantial meal in the honeysuckle arbour of the old inn garden, and the fashionable teas then going on in crowded drawing-rooms in town, where people hurried in, took a tiny roll of thin bread-and-butter, and a sip at luke-warm tea, which had stood sufficiently long to leave an abiding taste of tannin; heard or imparted a few more or less detrimental facts concerning mutual friends; then hurried on

43

elsewhere, to a cucumber sandwich, colder tea, which had stood even longer, and a fresh instalment of gossip.

"Oh, why do we do it?" mused Lady Ingleby. Then, taking up her scarlet parasol, she crossed the little lawn, and stood at the garden gate, in the afternoon sunlight, debating in which direction she should go.

Usually her walks took her along the top of the cliffs, where the larks, springing from the short turf and clumps of waving harebells, sang themselves up into the sky. She loved being high above the sea, and hearing the distant thunder of the breakers on the rocks below.

But to-day the steep little street, down through the fishing village, to the cove, looked inviting. The tide was out, and the sands gleamed golden.

Also, from her seat in the arbour, she had seen Jim Airth's tall figure go swinging along the cliff edge, silhouetted against the clear blue of the sky. And one sentence in the letter she had just received, made this into a factor which turned her feet toward the shore.

The friendly Cornish folk, sitting on their doorsteps in the sunshine, smiled at the lovely woman in white serge, who passed down their village street, so tall and graceful, beneath the shade of her scarlet parasol. An item in the doctor's prescription had been the discarding of widow's weeds, and it had seemed quite natural to Myra to come down to her first Cornish breakfast in a cream serge gown.

Arrived at the shore, she turned in the direction she usually took when up above, and walked quickly along the firm smooth sand; pausing occasionally to pick up a beautifully marked stone, or to examine a brilliant sea-anemone or gleaming jelly-fish, left stranded by the tide.

Presently she reached a place where the cliff jutted out toward the sea; and, climbing over slippery rocks, studded with shining pools in which crimson seaweed waved, crabs scudded sideways from her passing shadow, and darting shrimps flicked across and buried themselves hastily in the sand, Myra found herself in a most fascinating cove. The line of cliff here made a horseshoe, not quite half a mile in length. The little bay, within this curve, was a place of almost fairy-like beauty; the sand a soft glistening white, decked with delicate crimson seaweed. The cliffs, towering up above, gave welcome shadow to the shore; yet the sun behind them still gleamed and sparkled on the distant sea.

Myra walked to the centre of the horseshoe; then, picking up a piece of driftwood, scooped out a comfortable hollow in the sand, about a dozen yards from the foot of the cliff; stuck her open parasol up behind it, to shield herself from the observation, from above, of any chance passer-by; and, settling comfortably into the soft hollow, lay back, watching, through half-closed lids, the fleeting shadows, the blue sky, the gently moving sea. Little white clouds blushed rosy red. An opal tint gleamed on the water. The moving ripple seemed too far away to break the restful silence.

Lady Ingleby's eyelids drooped lower and lower.

"Yes, my dear Jane," she murmured, dreamily watching a snow-white sail, as it rounded the point, curtseyed, and vanished from view; "undoubtedly a—a well-expressed sentence; but far from—from—being fact. The safely abstract could hardly require—a—a—a cameo——"

The long walk, the sea breeze, the distant lapping of the water—all these combined had done their soothing work.

Lady Ingleby slept peacefully in Horseshoe Cove; and the rising tide crept in.

CHAPTER IX

JIM AIRTH TO THE RESCUE

An hour later, a man swung along the path at the summit of the cliffs, whistling like a blackbird.

The sun was setting; and, as he walked, he revelled in the gold and crimson of the sky; in the opal tints upon the heaving sea.

The wind had risen as the sun set, and breakers were beginning to pound along the shore.

Suddenly something caught his eye, far down below.

"By Jove!" he said. "A scarlet poppy on the sands!"

He walked on, until his rapid stride brought him to the centre of the cliff above Horseshoe Cove.

Then—"Good Lord!" said Jim Airth, and stood still.

He had caught sight of Lady Ingleby's white skirt reposing on the sand, beyond the scarlet parasol.

"Good Lord!" said Jim Airth.

Then he scanned the horizon. Not a boat to be seen.

His quick eye travelled along the cliff, the way he had come. Not a living thing in sight.

On to the fishing village. Faint threads of ascending vapour indicated chimneys. "Two miles at least," muttered Jim Airth. "I could not run it and get back with a boat, under three quarters of an hour."

Then he looked down into the cove.

"Both ends cut off. The water will reach her feet in ten minutes; will sweep the base of the cliff, in twenty."

Exactly beneath the spot where he stood, more than half way down, was a ledge about six feet long by four feet wide.

Letting himself over the edge, holding to tufts of grass, tiny shrubs, jutting stones, cracks in the surface of the sandstone, he managed to reach this narrow ledge, dropping the last ten feet, and landing on it by an almost superhuman effort of balance.

One moment he paused; carefully took its measure; then, leaning over, looked down. Sixty feet remained, a precipitous slope, with nothing to which foot could hold, or hand could cling.

Jim Airth buttoned his Norfolk jacket, and tightened his belt. Then slipping, feet foremost off the ledge, he glissaded down on his back, bending his knees at the exact moment when his feet thudded heavily on to the sand.

For a moment the shock stunned him. Then he got up and looked around.

He stood, within ten yards of the scarlet parasol, on the small strip of sand still left uncovered by the rapidly advancing sweep of the rising tide.

CHAPTER X

"YEO HO, WE GO!"

"A cameo chaperonage," murmured Lady Ingleby, and suddenly opened her eyes.

Sky and sea were still there, but between them, closer than sea or sky, looking down upon her with a tense light in his blue eyes, stood Jim Airth.

"Why, I have been asleep!" said Lady Ingleby.

"You have," said Jim Airth; "and meanwhile the sun has set, and—the tide has come up. Allow me to assist you to rise."

Lady Ingleby put her hand into his, and he helped her to her feet. She stood beside him gazing, with wide startled eyes, at the expanse of sea, the rushing waves, the tiny strip of sand.

"The tide seems very high," said Lady Ingleby.

"Very high," agreed Jim Airth. He stood close beside her, but his eyes still eagerly scanned the water. If by any chance a boat came round the point there would still be time to hail it.

"We seem to be cut off," said Lady Ingleby.

"We are cut off," replied Jim Airth, laconically.

"Then I suppose we must have a boat," said Lady Ingleby.

"An excellent suggestion," replied Jim Airth, drily, "if a boat were to be had. But, unfortunately, we are two miles from the hamlet, and this is not a time when boats pass in and out; nor would they come this way. When I saw you, from the top of the cliff, I calculated the chances as to whether I could reach the boats, and be back here in time. But, before I could have returned with a boat, you would have—been very wet," finished Jim Airth, somewhat lamely.

He looked at the lovely face, close to his shoulder. It was pale and serious, but showed no sign of fear.

He glanced at the point of cliff beyond. Twenty feet above its rocky base the breakers were dashing; but round that point would be safety.

"Can you swim?" asked Jim Airth, eagerly.

Myra's calm grey eyes met his, steadily. A gleam of amusement dawned in them.

"If you put your hand under my chin, and count 'one—two! one—two!' very loud and quickly, I can swim nearly ten yards," she said.

Jim Airth laughed. His eyes met hers, in sudden comprehending comradeship. "By Jove, you're plucky!" they seemed to say. But what he really said was: "Then swimming is no go."

"No go, for me," said Myra, earnestly, "nor for you, weighted by me. We should never get round that eddying whirlpool. It would merely mean that we should both be drowned. But you can easily do it alone. Oh, go at once! Go quickly! And—don't look back. I shall be all right. I shall just sit down against the cliff, and wait. I have always been fond of the sea."

Jim Airth looked at her again. And, this time, open admiration shone in his keen eyes.

"Ah, brave!" he said. "A mother of soldiers! Such women make of us a fighting race."

Myra laid her hand on his sleeve. "My friend," she said, "it was never given me to be a mother. But I am a soldier's daughter, and a soldier's widow; and—I am not afraid to die. Oh, I do beg of you— give me one handclasp and go!"

Jim Airth took the hand held out, but he kept it firmly in his own.

"You shall not die," he said, between his teeth. "Do you suppose I would leave any woman to die alone? And you—you, of all women!—By heaven," he repeated, doggedly; "you shall not die. Do you think I could go; and leave—" he broke off abruptly.

Myra smiled. His hand was very strong, and her heart felt strangely restful. And had he not said: "You, of all women?" But, even in what seemed likely to be her last moments, Lady Ingleby's unfailing instinct was to be tactful.

"I am sure you would leave no woman in danger," she said; "and some, alas! might have been easier to save than I. Plump little Miss Susie would have floated."

Jim Airth's big laugh rang out. "And Miss Murgatroyd could have sailed away in her cameo," he said.

Then, as if that laugh had broken the spell which held him inactive: "Come," he cried, and drew her to the foot of the cliff; "we have not a moment to lose! Look! Do you see the way I came down? See that long slide in the sand? I tobogganed down there on my back. Pretty steep, and nothing to hold to, I admit; but not so very far up, after all. And, where my slide begins, is a blessed ledge four foot by six." He pulled out a huge clasp-knife, opened the largest blade, and commenced hacking steps in the face of the cliff. "We must climb," said Jim Airth.

"I have never climbed," whispered Myra's voice behind him.

"You must climb to-day," said Jim Airth.

"I could never even climb trees," whispered Myra.

"You must climb a cliff to-night. It is our only chance."

He hacked on, rapidly.

Suddenly he paused. "Show me your reach," he said. "Mine would not do. Put your left hand there; so. Now stretch up with your right; as high as you can, easily.... Ah! three foot six, or thereabouts. Now your left foot close to the bottom. Step up with your right, as high as you can comfortably.... Two foot, nine. Good! One step, more or less, might make all the difference, by-and-by. Now listen, while I work. What a God-send for us that there happens to be, just here, this stratum of soft sand. We should have been done for, had the cliff been serpentine marble. You must choose between two plans. I could scrape you a step, wider than the rest—almost a ledge—just out of reach of the water, leaving you there, while I go on up, and finish. Then I could return for you. You could climb in front, I helping from below. You would feel safer. Or—you must follow me up now, step by step, as I cut them."

"I could not wait on a ledge alone," said Myra. "I will follow you, step by step."

"Good," said Jim Airth; "it will save time. I am afraid you must take off your shoes and stockings. Nothing will do for this work, but naked feet. We shall need to stick our toes into the sand, and make them cling on like fingers."

He pulled off his own boots and stockings; then drew the belt from his Norfolk jacket, and fastened it firmly round his left ankle in such a way that a long end would hang down behind him as he mounted.

"See that?" he said. "When you are in the niches below me, it will hang close to your hands. If you are slipping, and feel you must clutch at something, catch hold of that. Only, if possible, shout first, and I will stick on like a limpet, and try to withstand the strain. But don't do it, unless really necessary."

He picked up Myra's shoes and stockings, and put them into his big pockets.

At that moment an advance wave rushed up the sand and caught their bare feet.

"Oh, Jim Airth," cried Myra, "go without me! I have not a steady head. I cannot climb."

He put his hands upon her shoulders, and looked full into her eyes.

"You can climb," he said. "You must climb. You shall climb. We must climb—or drown. And, remember; if you fall, I fall too. You will not be saving me, by letting yourself go."

She looked up into his eyes, despairingly. They blazed into hers from beneath his bent brows. She felt the tremendous mastery of his will. Her own gave one final struggle.

"I have nothing to live for, Jim Airth," she said. "I am alone in the world."

"So am I," he cried. "I have been worse than alone, for a half score of years. But there is life to live for. Would you throw away the highest of all gifts? I want to live—Good God! I must live; and so must you. We live or die together."

He loosed her shoulders and took her by the wrists. He lifted her trembling hands, and held them against his breast.

For a moment they stood so, in absolute silence.

Then Myra felt herself completely dominated. All fear slipped from her; but the assurance which took its place was his courage, not hers; and she knew it. Lifting her head, she smiled at him, with white lips.

"I shall not fall," she said.

Another wave swept round their ankles, and remained there.

"Good," said Jim Airth, and loosed her wrists. "We shall owe our lives to each other. Next time I look into your face, please God, we shall be in safety. Come!"

He sprang up the face of the cliff, standing in the highest niches he had made.

"Now follow me, carefully," he said; "slowly, and carefully. We are not in a position to hurry. Always keep each hand and each foot firmly in a niche. Are you there? Good!... Now don't look either up or down, but keep your eyes on my heels. Directly I move, come on into the empty places. See?... Now then. Can you manage?... Good! On we go! After all it won't take long.... I say, what fun if the Miss Murgatroyds peeped over the cliff! Amelia would be so shocked at our bare feet. Eliza would cry: 'Oh my dear love!' And Susie would promptly fall upon us! Hullo! Steady down there! Don't laugh too much.... Fine knife, this. I bought it in Mexico. And if the big blade gives out, there are two more; also a saw, and a corkscrew.... Mind the falling sand does not get into your eyes.... Tell me if the niches are not deep enough, and remember there is no hurry, we are not aiming to catch any particular train! Steady down there! Don't laugh.... Up we go! Oh, good! This is a third of the way. Don't look either up or down. Watch my heels—I wish they were more worth looking at—and remember the belt is quite handy, and I am as firm as a rock up here. You and all the Miss Murgatroyds might hang on to it together. Steady down there!... All right; I won't mention them.... By the way, the water must be fairly deep below us now. If you fell, you would merely get a ducking. I should slide down and pull you out, and we would start afresh.... Good Lord!... Oh, never mind! Nothing. Only, my knife slipped, but I caught it again.... We must be half way, by now. How lucky we have my

51

glissading marks to guide us. I can't see the ledge from here. Let's sing 'Nancy Lee.' I suppose you know it. I can always work better to a good rollicking tune."

Then, as he drove his blade into the cliff, Jim Airth's gay voice rang out:

> "Of all the wives as e'er you know,
> Yeo ho! lads! ho!
> Yeo ho! Yeo ho!
> There's none like Nancy Lee, I trow,
> Yeo ho! lads! ho!
> Yeo ho!
> See there she stands

—Blow! I've struck a rock! Not a big one though. Remember this step will be slightly more to your right

> —and waves her hands,
> Upon the quay,
> And ev'ry day when I'm away,
> She'll watch for me;
> And whisper low, when tempests blow—

Oh, hang these unexpected stones! That's finished my big blade!

> —For Jack at sea,
> Yeo ho! lads, ho! Yeo ho!

Now the chorus.

> The sailor's wife the sailor's star shall be,—

Come on! You sing too!"

> "Yeo ho! we go,
> Across the sea!"

came Lady Ingleby's voice from below, rather faint and quavering.

"That's right!" shouted Jim Airth. "Keep it up! I can see the ledge now, just above us.

> The bo's'n pipes the watch below,
> Yeo ho! lads! ho!

52

Yeo ho! Yeo ho!
Then here's a health afore we go,
Yeo ho! lads! ho!
Yeo ho!
A long, long life to my sweet wife,
And mates at sea

—Keep it up down there! I have one hand on the ledge—

And keep our bones from Davy Jones
Where'er we be!"
"And—keep our bones—from—
Davy Jones—who e'er he be,"

quavered Lady Ingleby, making one final effort to move up into the vacant niches, though conscious that her fingers and toes were so numb that she could not feel them grip the sand.

Then Jim Airth's whole body vanished suddenly from above her, as he drew himself on to the ledge.

"Yeo ho! we go!" Came his gay voice from above.

"Yeo ho! Yeo ho!"

sang Lady Ingleby, in a faint whisper.

She could not move on into the empty niches. She could only remain where she was, clinging to the face of the cliff.

She suddenly thought of a fly on a wall; and remembered a particular fly, years ago, on her nursery wall. She had followed its ascent with a small interested finger, and her nurse had come by with a duster, and saying: "Nasty thing!" had ruthlessly flicked it off. The fly had fallen—fallen dead, on the nursery carpet.... Lady Ingleby felt she too was falling. She gave one agonised glance upward to the towering cliff, with the line of sky above it. Then everything swayed and rocked. "A mother of soldiers," her brain insisted, "must fall without screaming." Then—A long arm shot down from above; a strong hand gripped her firmly.

"One step more," said Jim Airth's voice, close to her ear, "and I can lift you."

She made the effort, and he drew her on to the ledge beside him.

"Thank you very much," said Lady Ingleby. "And who was Davy Jones?"

Jim Airth's face was streaming with perspiration. His mouth was full of sand. His heart was beating in his throat. But he loved to

53

play the game, and he loved to see another do it. So he laughed as he put his arm around her, holding her tightly so that she should not realise how much she was trembling.

"Davy Jones," he said, "is a gentleman who has a locker at the bottom of the sea, into which all drown'd things go. I am afraid your pretty parasol has gone there, and my boots and stockings. But we may well spare him those.... Oh, I say!.... Yes, do have a good cry. Don't mind me. And don't you think between us we could remember some sort of a prayer? For if ever two people faced death together, we have faced it; and, by God's mercy, here we are—alive."

CHAPTER XI

'TWIXT SEA AND SKY

Myra never forgot Jim Airth's prayer. Instinctively she knew it to be the first time he had voiced his soul's thanksgiving or petitions in the presence of another. Also she realised that, for the first time in her whole life, prayer became to her a reality. As she crouched on the ledge beside him, shaking uncontrollably, so that, but for his arm about her, she must have lost her balance and fallen; as she heard that strong soul expressing in simple unorthodox language its gratitude for life and safety, mingled with earnest petition for keeping through the night and complete deliverance in the morning; it seemed to Myra that the heavens opened, and the felt presence of God surrounded them in their strange isolation.

An immense peace filled her. By the time those disjointed halting sentences were finished, Myra had ceased trembling; and when Jim Airth, suddenly at a loss how else to wind up his prayer, commenced "Our Father, Who art in heaven," Myra's sweet voice united with his, full of an earnest fervour of petition.

At the final words, Jim Airth withdrew his arm, and a shy silence fell between them. The emotion of the mind had awakened an awkwardness of body. In that uniting "Our Father," their souls had leapt on, beyond where their bodies were quite prepared to follow.

Lady Ingleby saved the situation. She turned to Jim Airth, with that impulsive sweetness which could never be withstood. In the rapidly deepening twilight, he could just see the large wistful grey eyes, in the white oval of her face.

"Do you know," she said, "I really couldn't possibly sit all night, on a ledge the size of a Chesterfield sofa, with a person I had to call 'Mr.' I could only sit there with an old and intimate friend, who would naturally call me 'Myra,' and whom I might call 'Jim.' Unless I may call you 'Jim,' I shall insist on climbing down and swimming home. And if you address me as 'Mrs. O'Mara,' I shall certainly become hysterical, and tumble off!"

"Why of course," said Jim Airth. "I hate titles of any kind. I come of an old Quaker stock, and plain names with no prefixes always seem best to me. And are we not old and trusted friends? Was not each of those minutes on the face of the cliff, a year? While that second which elapsed between the slipping of my knife from my right hand and the catching of it, against my knee, by my left, may go at ten years! Ah, think if it had dropped altogether! No, don't think. We were barely half way up. Now you must contrive to put on your shoes and stockings." He produced them from his pocket. "And then we must find out how to place ourselves most comfortably and safely. We have but one enemy to fight during the next seven hours—cramp. You must tell me immediately if you feel it threatening anywhere, I have done a lot of scouting in my time, and know a dodge or two. I also know what it is to lie in one position for hours, not daring to move a muscle, the cold sweat pouring off my face, simply from the agonies of cramp. We must guard against that."

"Jim," said Myra, "how long shall we have to sit here?"

He made a quick movement, as if the sound of his name from her lips for the first time, meant much to him; and there was in his voice an added depth of joyousness, as he answered:

"It would be impossible to climb from here to the top of the cliff. When I came down, I had a sheer drop of ten feet. You see the cliff slightly overhangs just above us. So far as the tide is concerned we might clamber down in three hours; but there is no moon, and by then, it will be pitch dark. We must have light for our descent, if I am to land you safe and unshaken at the bottom. Dawn should be breaking soon after three. The sun rises to-morrow at .; but it will be quite light before then. I think we may expect to reach the Moorhead Inn by A.M. Let us hope Miss Murgatroyd will not be looking out of her window, as we stroll up the path."

"What are they all thinking now?" questioned Lady Ingleby.

"I don't know, and I don't care," said Jim Airth, gaily. "You're alive, and I'm alive; and we've done a record climb! Nothing else matters."

"No, but seriously, Jim?"

"Well, seriously, it is very unlikely that I shall be missed at all. I often dine elsewhere, and let myself in quite late; or stop out altogether. How about you?"

"Why, curiously enough," said Myra, "before coming out I locked my bedroom door. I have the key here. I had left some papers lying about—I am not a very tidy person. On the only other occasion upon which I locked my door, I omitted dinner altogether, and went to bed on returning from my evening walk. I am supposed to be doing a 'rest-cure' here. The maid tried my door, went away, and did not turn up again until next morning. Most likely she has done the same to-night."

"Then I don't suppose they will send out a search-party," said Jim Airth.

"No. We are so alone down here. We only matter to ourselves," said Myra.

"And to each other," said Jim Airth, quietly.

Myra's heart stood still.

Those four words, spoken so simply by that deep tender voice, meant more to her than any words had ever meant. They meant so much, that they made for themselves a silence—a vast holy temple of wonder and realisation wherein they echoed back and forth, repeating themselves again and again.

The two on the ledge sat listening.

The chant of mutual possession, so suddenly set going, was too beautiful a thing to be interrupted by other words.

Even Lady Ingleby's unfailing habit of tactful speech was not allowed to spoil the deep sweetness of this unexpected situation. Myra's heart was waking; and when the heart is stirred, the mind sometimes forgets to be tactful.

At length:—"Don't you remember," he said, very low, "what I told you before we began to climb? Did I not say, that if we succeeded in reaching the ledge safely, we should owe our lives to each other? Well, we did; and—we do."

"Ah, no," cried Myra, impulsively. "No, Jim Airth! You—glad, and safe, and free—were walking along the top of these cliffs. I, in my senseless folly, lay sleeping on the sand below, while the tide rose around me. You came down into danger to save me, risking your life in so doing. I owe you my life, Jim Airth; you owe me nothing."

The man beside her turned and looked at her, with his quiet whimsical smile.

"I am not accustomed to have my statements amended," he said, drily.

It was growing so dark, they could only just discern each other's faces.

Lady Ingleby laughed. She was so unused to that kind of remark, that, at the moment she could frame no suitable reply.

Presently:—"I suppose I really owe my life to my scarlet parasol," she said. "Had it not attracted your attention, you would not have seen me."

"Should I not?" questioned Jim Airth, his eyes on the white loveliness of her face. "Since I saw you first, on the afternoon of your arrival, have you ever once come within my range of vision without my seeing you, and taking in every detail?"

"On the afternoon of my arrival?" questioned Lady Ingleby, astonished.

"Yes," replied Jim Airth, deliberately. "Seven o'clock, on the

57

first of June. I stood at the smoking-room window, at a loose end of all things; sick of myself, dissatisfied with my manuscript, tired of fried fish—don't laugh; small things, as well as great, go to make up the sum of a man's depression. Then the gate swung back, and YOU—in golden capitals—the sunlight in your eyes, came up the garden path. I judged you to be a woman grown, in years perhaps not far short of my own age; I guessed you a woman of the world, with a position to fill, and a knowledge of men and things. Yet you looked just a lovely child, stepping into fairy-land; the joyful surprise of unexpected holiday danced in your radiant eyes. Since then, the beautiful side of life has always been you—YOU, in golden capitals."

Jim Airth paused, and sat silent.

It was quite dark now.

Myra slipped her hand into his, which closed upon it with a strong unhesitating clasp.

"Go on, Jim," she said, softly.

"I went out into the hall, and saw your name in the visitors' book. The ink was still wet. The handwriting was that of the holiday-child—I should like to set you copies! The name surprised me—agreeably. I had expected to be able at once to place the woman who had walked up the path. It was a surprise and a relief to find that my Fairy-land Princess was not after all a fashionable beauty or a society leader, but owned just a simple Irish name, and lived at a Lodge."

"Go on, Jim," said Lady Ingleby, rather tremulously.

"Then the name 'Shenstone' interested me, because I know the Inglebys—at least, I knew Lord Ingleby, well; and I shall soon know Lady Ingleby. In fact I have written to-day asking for an interview. I must see her on business connected with notes of her husband's which, if she gives permission, are to be embodied in my book. I suppose if you live near Shenstone Park you know the Inglebys?"

"Yes," said Myra. "But tell me, Jim; if—if you noticed so much that first day; if you were—interested; if you wanted to set me copies—yes, I know I write a shocking hand;—why would you never look at me? Why were you so stiff and unfriendly? Why were you not as nice to me as you were to Susie, for instance?"

Jim Airth sat long in silence, staring out into the darkness. At last he said:

"I want to tell you. Of course, I must tell you. But—may I ask a few questions first?"

Lady Ingleby also gazed unseeingly into the darkness; but she leaned a little nearer to the broad shoulder beside her. "Ask me

58

what you will," she said. "There is nothing, in my whole life, I would not tell you, Jim Airth."

Her cheek was so close to the rough Norfolk jacket, that if it had moved a shade nearer, she would have rested against it. But it did not move; only, the clasp on her hand tightened.

"Were you married very young?" asked Jim Airth.

"I was not quite eighteen. It is ten years ago."

"Did you marry for love?"

There was a long silence, while both looked steadily into the darkness.

Then Myra answered, speaking very slowly. "To be quite honest, I think I married chiefly to escape from a very unhappy home. Also I was very young, and knew nothing—nothing of life, and nothing of love; and—how can I explain, Jim Airth?—I have not learnt much during these ten long years."

"Have you been unhappy?" He asked the question very low.

"Not exactly unhappy. My husband was a very good man; kind and patient, beyond words, towards me. But I often vaguely felt I was missing the Best in life. Now—I know I was."

"How long have you been—How long has he been dead?" The deep voice was so tender, that the question could bring no pain.

"Seven months," replied Lady Ingleby. "My husband was killed in the assault on Targai."

"At Targai!" exclaimed Jim Airth, surprised into betraying his astonishment. Then at once recovering himself: "Ah, yes; of course. Seven months. I was there, you know."

But, within himself, he was thinking rapidly, and much was becoming clear.

Sergeant O'Mara! Was it possible? An exquisite refined woman such as this, bearing about her the unmistakable hall-mark of high birth and perfect breeding? The Sergeant was a fine fellow, and superior—but, good Lord! Her husband! Yet girls of eighteen do foolish things, and repent ever after. A runaway match from an unhappy home; then cast off by her relations, and now left friendless and alone. But—Sergeant O'Mara! Yet no other O'Mara fell at Targai; and there was some link between him and Lord Ingleby.

Then, into his musing, came Myra's soft voice, from close beside him, in the darkness: "My husband was always good to me; but——"

And Jim Airth laid his other hand over the one he held. "I am sure he was," he said, gently. "But if you had been older, and had known more of love and life you would have done differently. Don't try to explain. I understand."

59

And Myra gladly left it at that. It would have been so very difficult to explain further, without explaining Michael; and all that really mattered was, that—with or without explanation—Jim Airth understood.

"And now—tell me," she suggested, softly.

"Ah, yes," he said, pulling himself together, with an effort. "My experience also misses the Best, and likewise covers ten long years. But it is a harder one than yours. I married, when a boy of twenty-one, a woman, older than myself; supremely beautiful. I went mad over her loveliness. Nothing seemed to count or matter, but that. I knew she was not a good woman, but I thought she might become so; and even if she didn't it made no difference. I wanted her. Afterwards I found she had laughed at me, all the time. Also, there had all the time been another—an older man than I—who had laughed with her. He had not been in a position to marry her when I did; but two years later, he came into money. Then—she left me."

Jim Airth paused. His voice was hard with pain. The night was very black. In the dark silence they could hear the rhythmic thunder of the waves pounding monotonously against the cliff below.

"I divorced her, of course; and he married her; but I went abroad, and stayed abroad. I never could look upon her as other than my wife. She had made a hell of my life; robbed me of every illusion; wrecked my ideals; imbittered my youth. But I had said, before God, that I took her for my wife, until death parted us; and, so long as we were both alive, what power could free me from that solemn oath? It seemed to me that by remaining in another hemisphere, I made her second marriage less sinful. Often, at first, I was tempted to shoot myself, as a means of righting this other wrong. But in time I outgrew that morbidness, and realised that though Love is good, Life is the greatest gift of all. To throw it away, voluntarily, is an unpardonable sin. The suicide's punishment should be loss of immortality. Well, I found work to do, of all sorts, in America, and elsewhere. And a year ago—she died. I should have come straight home, only I was booked for that muddle on the frontier they called 'a war.' I got fever after Targai; was invalided home; and here I am recruiting and finishing my book. Now you can understand why loveliness in a woman, fills me with a sort of panic, even while a part of me still leaps up instinctively to worship it. I had often said to myself that if I ever ventured upon matrimony again, it should be a plain face, and a noble heart; though all the while I knew I should never bring myself really to want the plain face. And yet, just as the burnt child dreads the fire, I have always tried to look away from beauty. Only—my Fairy-land Princess, may I say it?—days ago I began to feel certain that in you—YOU in

60

golden capitals—the loveliness and the noble heart went together. But from the moment when, stepping out of the sunset, you walked up the garden path, right into my heart, the fact of YOU, just being what you are, and being here, meant so much to me, that I did not dare let it mean more. Somehow I never connected you with widowhood; and not until you said this evening on the shore: 'I am a soldier's widow,' did I know that you were free.—There! Now you have heard all there is to hear. I made a bad mistake at the beginning; but I hope I am not the sort of chap you need mind sitting on a ledge with, and calling 'Jim'."

For answer, Myra's cheek came trustfully to rest against the sleeve of the rough tweed coat. "Jim," she said; "Oh, Jim!"

Presently: "So you know the Inglebys?" remarked Jim Airth.

"Yes," said Myra.

"Is 'The Lodge' near Shenstone Park?"

"The Lodge is in the park. It is not at any of the gates.—I am not a gate-keeper, Jim!—It is a pretty little house, standing by itself, just inside the north entrance."

"Do you rent it from them?"

Myra hesitated, but only for the fraction of a second. "No; it is my own. Lord Ingleby gave it to me."

"Lord Ingleby?" Jim Airth's voice sounded like knitted brows. "Why not Lady Ingleby?"

"It was not hers, to give. All that is hers, was his."

"I see. Which of them did you know first?"

"I have known Lady Ingleby all my life," said Myra, truthfully; "and I have known Lord Ingleby since his marriage."

"Ah. Then he became your friend, because he married her?"

Myra laughed. "Yes," she said. "I suppose so."

"What's the joke?"

"Only that it struck me as an amusing way of putting it; but it is undoubtedly true."

"Have they any children?"

Myra's voice shook slightly. "No, none. Why do you ask?"

"Well, in the campaign, I often shared Lord Ingleby's tent; and he used to talk in his sleep."

"Yes?"

"There was one name he often called and repeated."

Lady Ingleby's heart stood still.

"Yes?" she said, hardly breathing.

"It was 'Peter'," continued Jim Airth. "The night before he was killed, he kept turning in his sleep and saying: 'Peter! Hullo, little Peter! Come here!' I thought perhaps he had a little son named Peter."

"He had no son," said Lady Ingleby, controlling her voice with effort. "Peter was a dog of which he was very fond. Was that the only name he spoke?"

"The only one I ever heard," replied Jim Airth.

Then suddenly Lady Ingleby clasped both hands round his arm.

"Jim," she whispered, brokenly, "Not once have you spoken my name. It was a bargain. We were to be old and intimate friends. I seem to have been calling you 'Jim' all my life! But you have not yet called me 'Myra,' Let me hear it now, please."

Jim Airth laid his big hand over both of hers.

"I can't," he said. "Hush! I can't. Not up here—it means too much. Wait until we get back to earth again. Then—Oh, I say! Can't you help?"

This kind of emotion was an unknown quantity to Lady Ingleby. So was the wild beating of her own heart. But she knew the situation called for tact, and was not tactful speech always her special forte?

"Jim," she said, "are you not frightfully hungry? I should be; only I had an enormous tea before coming out. Would you like to hear what I had for tea? No. I am afraid it would make you feel worse. I suppose dinner at the inn was over, long ago. I wonder what variation of fried fish they had, and whether Miss Susannah choked over a fish-bone, and had to be requested to leave the room. Oh, do you remember that evening? You looked so dismayed and alarmed, I quite thought you were going to the rescue! I wonder what time it is?"

"We can soon tell that," said Jim Airth, cheerfully. He dived into his pocket, produced a matchbox which he had long been fingering turn about with his pipe and tobacco-pouch, struck a light, and looked at his watch. Myra saw the lean brown face, in the weird flare of the match. She also saw the horrid depth so close to them, which she had almost forgotten. A sense of dizziness came over her. She longed to cling to his arm; but he had drawn it resolutely away.

"Half past ten," said Jim Airth. "Miss Murgatroyd has donned her night-cap. Miss Eliza has sighed: 'Good-night, summer, good-night, good-night,' at her open lattice; and Susie, folding her plump hands, has said: 'Now I lay me.'"

Myra laughed. "And they will all be listening for you to dump out your big boots," she said. "That is always your 'Good-night' to the otherwise silent house."

"No, really? Does it make a noise?" said Jim Airth, ruefully. "Never again——?"

"Oh, but you must," said Myra. "I love—I mean Susie loves the

62

sound, and listens for it. Jim, that match reminds me:—why don't you smoke? Surely it would help the hunger, and be comfortable and cheering."

Jim Airth's pipe and pouch were out in a twinkling.

"Sure you don't mind? It doesn't make you sick, or give you a headache?"

"No, I think I like it," said Myra. "In fact, I am sure I like it. That is, I like to sit beside it. No, I don't do it myself."

Another match flared, and again she saw the chasm, and the nearness of the edge. She bore it until the pipe was drawing well. Then: "Oh, Jim," she said, "I am so sorry; but I am afraid I am becoming dizzy. I feel as though I must fall over." She gave a half sob.

Jim Airth turned, instantly alert.

"Nonsense," he said, but the sharp word sounded tender. "Four good feet of width are as safe as forty. Change your position a bit." He put his arm around her, and moved her so that she leant more completely against the cliff at their backs. "Now forget the edge," he said, "and listen. I am going to tell you camp yarns, and tales of the Wild West."

Then as they sat on in the darkness, Jim Airth smoked and talked, painting vivid word-pictures of life and adventure in other lands. And Myra listened, absorbed and enchanted; every moment realising more fully, as he unconsciously revealed it, the manly strength and honest simplicity of his big nature, with its fun and its fire; its huge capacity for enjoyment; its corresponding capacity for pain.

And, as she listened, her heart said: "Oh, my cosmopolitan cowboy! Thank God you found no title in the book, to put you off. Thank God you found no name which you could 'place,' relegating its poor possessor to the ranks of 'society leaders' in which you would have had no share. And, oh! most of all, I thank God for the doctor's wise injunction: 'Leave behind you your own identity'!"

CHAPTER XII

UNDER THE MORNING STAR

The night wore on.

Stars shone in the deep purple sky; bright watchful eyes looking down unwearied upon the sleeping world.

The sound of the sea below fell from a roar to a murmur, and drew away into the distance.

It was a warm June night, and very still.

Jim Airth had moved along the ledge to the further end, and sat swinging his legs over the edge. His content was so deep and full, that ordinary speech seemed impossible; and silence, a glad necessity. The prospect of that which the future might hold in store, made the ledge too narrow to contain him. He sought relief in motion, and swung his long legs out into the darkness.

It had not occurred to him to wonder at his companion's silence; the reason for his own had been so all-sufficient.

At length he struck a match to see the time; then, turning with a smile, held it so that its light illumined Myra.

She knelt upon the ledge, her hands pressed against the overhanging cliff, her head turned in terror away from it. Her face was ashen in its whiteness, and large tears rolled down her cheeks.

Jim dropped the match, with an exclamation, and groped towards her in the darkness.

"Dear!" he cried, "Oh, my dear, what is the matter? Selfish fool, that I am! I thought you were just resting, quiet and content."

His groping hands found and held her.

"Oh, Jim," sobbed Lady Ingleby, "I am so sorry! It is so weak and unworthy. But I am afraid I feel faint. The whole cliff seems to rock and move. Every moment I fear it will tip me over. And you seemed miles away!"

"You are faint," said Jim Airth; "and no wonder. There is nothing weak or unworthy about it. You have been quite splendid. It is I who have been a thoughtless ass. But I can't have you fainting up here. You must lie down at once. If I sit on the edge with my back to you, can you slip along behind me and lie at full length, leaning against the cliff?"

"No, oh no, I couldn't!" whispered Myra. "It frightens me so horribly when you hang your legs over the edge, and I can't bear to touch the cliff. It seems worse than the black emptiness. It rocks to and fro, and seems to push me over. Oh, Jim! What shall I do? Help me, help me!"

"You must lie down," said Jim Airth, between his teeth. "Here, wait a minute. Move out a little way. Don't be afraid. I have hold of you. Let me get behind you.... That's right. Now you are not touching the cliff. Let me get my shoulders firmly into the hollow at this end, and my feet fixed at the other. There! With my back rammed into it like this, nothing short of an earthquake could dislodge me. Now dear—turn your back to me and your face to the sea and let yourself go. You will not fall over. Do not be afraid."

Very gently, but very firmly, he drew her into his arms.

Tired, frightened, faint,—Lady Ingleby was conscious at first of nothing save the intense relief of the sense of his great strength about her. She seemed to have been fighting the cliff and resisting the gaping darkness, until she was utterly worn out. Now she yielded to his gentle insistence, and sank into safety. Her cheek rested against his rough coat, and it seemed to her more soothing than the softest pillow. With a sigh of content, she folded her hands upon her breast, and he laid one of his big ones firmly over them both. She felt so safe, and held.

Then she heard Jim Airth's voice, close to her ear.

"We are not alone," he said. "You must try to sleep, dear; but first I want you to realise that we are not alone. Do you know what I mean? God is here. When I was a very little chap, I used to go to a Dame-school in the Highlands; and the old dame made me learn by heart the hundred and thirty-ninth psalm. I have repeated parts of it in all sorts of places of difficulty and danger. I am going to say my favourite verses to you now. Listen. 'Whither shall I go from Thy Spirit? or whither shall I flee from Thy presence?... If I take the wings of the morning, and dwell in the uttermost parts of the sea; even there shall Thy hand lead me, and Thy right hand shall hold me. If I say, Surely the darkness shall cover me; even the night shall be light about me. Yea, the darkness hideth not from Thee; but the night shineth as the day: the darkness and the light are both alike to Thee.... How precious also are Thy thoughts unto me, O God! how great is the sum of them. If I should count them they are more in number than the sand: when I awake I am still with Thee.'"

The deep voice ceased. Lady Ingleby opened her eyes. "I was nearly asleep," she said. "How good you are, Jim."

"No, I am not good," he answered. "I'm a tough chap, full of faults, and beset by failings. Only—if you will trust me, please God, I will never fail you. But now I want you to sleep; and I don't want you to think about me. I am merely a thing, which by God's providence is allowed to keep you in safety. Do you see that wonderful planet, hanging like a lamp in the sky? Watch it, while I tell you some lines written by an American woman, on the thought of that last verse."

And with his cheek against her soft hair, and his strong arms firmly round her, Jim Airth repeated, slowly, Mrs. Beecher Stowe's matchless poem:

> "Still, still with Thee, when purple morning breaketh,
> When the bird waketh, and the shadows flee;
> Fairer than morning, lovelier than daylight,
> Dawns the sweet consciousness—I am with Thee.
>
> "Alone with Thee, amid the mystic shadows,
> The solemn hush of nature newly born;
> Alone with Thee, in breathless adoration,
> In the calm dew and freshness of the morn.
>
> "As in the dawning, o'er the waveless ocean,
> The image of the morning star doth rest;
> So in this stillness Thou beholdest only
> Thine image in the waters of my breast.
>
> "When sinks the soul, subdued by toil, to slumber
> Its closing eye looks up to Thee in prayer;
> Sweet the repose, beneath Thy wings o'ershadowing,
> But sweeter still to wake, and find Thee there.
>
> "So shall it be at last, in that bright morning
> When the soul waketh, and life's shadows flee;
> Oh, in that hour, fairer than daylight's dawning,
> Shall rise the glorious thought, I am with Thee!"

Jim Airth's voice ceased. He waited a moment in silence. Then—"Do you like it?" he asked softly.

There was no answer. Myra slept as peacefully as a little child. He could feel the regular motion of her quiet breathing, beneath his hand.

"Thank God!" said Jim Airth, with his eyes on the morning star.

CHAPTER XIII

THE AWAKENING

When Lady Ingleby opened her eyes, she could not, for a moment, imagine where she was.

Dawn was breaking over the sea. A rift of silver, in the purple sky, had taken the place of the morning star. She could see the silvery gleam reflected in the ocean.

"Why am I sleeping so close to a large window?" queried her bewildered mind. "Or am I on a balcony?"

"Why do I feel so extraordinarily strong and rested?" questioned her slowly awakening body.

She lay quite still and considered the matter.

Then looking down, she saw a large brown hand clasping both hers. Her head was resting in the curve of the arm to which the hand belonged. A strong right arm was flung over and around her. All questionings were solved by two short words: "Jim Airth."

Lady Ingleby lay very still. She feared to break the deep spell of restfulness which held her. She hesitated to bring down to earth the exquisite sense of heaven, by which she was surrounded.

As the dawn broke over the sea, a wonderful light dawned in her eyes, a radiance such as had never shone in those sweet eyes before. "Dear God," she whispered, "am I to know the Best?"

Then she gently withdrew one hand, and laid it on the hand which had covered both.

"Jim," she said. "Jim! Look! It is day."

"Yes?" came Jim Airth's voice from behind her. "Yes? What? come in!—Hullo! Oh, I say!"

Myra smiled into the dawning. She had already come through those first moments of astonished realisation. But Jim Airth awoke to the situation more quickly than she had done.

"Hullo!" he said. "I meant to keep watch all the time; but I must have slept. Are you all right? Sure? No cramp? Well, I have a cramp in my left leg which will make me kick down the cliff in another minute, if I don't move it. Let me help you up.... That's the way. Now you sit safely there, while I get unwedged.... By Jove! I believe I've grown into the cliff, like a fossil ichthyosaurus. Did you ever see an ichthyosaurus? Doesn't it seem years since you said: 'And who is Davy Jones?' Don't you want some breakfast? I suppose it's about time we went home."

Talking gaily all the time, Jim Airth drew up his long limbs, rubbing them vigorously; stretched his arms above his head; then passed his hand over his tumbled hair.

"My wig!" he said. "What a morning! And how good to be alive!"

Myra stole a look at him. His eyes were turned seaward. The same dawn-light was in them, as shone in her own.

"Don't you want breakfast?" said Jim Airth, and pulled out his watch.

"I do," said Myra, gaily. "And now I can venture to tell you what delicious home-made bread I had for tea. What time is it, Jim?"

"Half past three. In a few minutes the sun will rise. Watch! Did you ever before see the dawn? Is it not wonderful? Always more of pearl and silver than at sunset. Look how the narrow rift has widened and spread right across the sky. The Monarch of Day is coming! See the little herald clouds, in livery of pink and gold. Now watch where the sea looks brightest. Ah!... There is the tip of his blood-red rim, rising out of the ocean. And how quickly the whole ball appears. Now see the rippling path of gold and crimson, a royal highway on the waters, right from the shore below us, to the footstool of his brilliant Majesty.... A new day has begun; and we have not said 'Good-morning.' Why should we? We did not say 'Good-night.' How ideal it would be, never to say 'Good-morning'; and never to say 'Good-night.' The night would be always 'good', and so would the morning. All life would be one grand crescendo of good—better—best. What? Have we found the Best? Ah, hush! I did not mean to say that yet.... Are you ready for the climb down? No, I can't allow any peeping over, and considering. If you really feel afraid of it, I will run to Tregarth as quickly as possible, rouse the sleeping village, bring ropes and men, and haul you up from the top."

"I absolutely decline to be 'hauled up from the top,' or to be left here alone," declared Lady Ingleby.

"Then the sooner we start down, the better," said Jim Airth. "I'm going first." He was over the edge before Myra could open her lips to expostulate. "Now turn round. Hold on to the ledge firmly with your hands, and give me your feet. Do you hear? Do as I tell you. Don't hesitate. It is less steep than it seemed yesterday. We are quite safe. Come on!... That's right."

Then Lady Ingleby passed through a most terrifying five minutes, while she yielded in blind obedience to the strong hands beneath her, and the big voice which encouraged and threatened alternately.

But when the descent was over and she stood on the shore

beside Jim Airth; when together they turned and looked in silence up the path of glory on the rippling waters, to the blazing beauty of the rising sun, thankful tears rushed to Lady Ingleby's eyes.

"Oh, Jim," she exclaimed, "God is good! It is so wonderful to be alive!"

Then Jim Airth turned, his face transfigured, the sunlight in his eyes, and opened his arms. "Myra," he said. "We have found the Best."

They walked along the shore, and up the steep street of the sleeping village, hand in hand like happy children.

Arrived at the Moorhead Inn, they pushed open the garden gate, and stepped noiselessly across the sunlit lawn.

The front door was firmly bolted. Jim Airth slipped round to the back, but returned in a minute shaking his head. Then he felt in his pocket for the big knife which had served them so well; pushed back the catch of the coffee-room window; softly raised the sash; swung one leg over, and drew Myra in after him.

Once in the familiar room, with its mustard-pots and salt-cellars, its table-cloths, left on in readiness for breakfast, they both lapsed into fits of uncontrollable laughter; laughter the more overwhelming, because it had to be silent.

Jim, recovering first, went off to the larder to forage for food.

Lady Ingleby flew noiselessly up to her room to wash her hands, and smooth her hair. She returned in two minutes to find Jim, very proud of his success, setting out a crusty home-made loaf, a large cheese, and a foaming tankard of ale.

Lady Ingleby longed for tea, and had never in her life drunk ale out of a pewter pot. But not for worlds would she have spoiled Jim Airth's boyish delight in the success of his raid on the larder.

So they sat at the centre table, Myra in Miss Murgatroyd's place, and Jim in Susie's, and consumed their bread-and-cheese, and drank their beer, with huge appetites and prodigious enjoyment. And Jim used Miss Susannah's napkin, and pretended to be sentimental over it. And Myra reproved him, after the manner of Miss Murgatroyd reproving Susie. After which they simultaneously exclaimed: "Oh, my dear love!" in Miss Eliza's most affecting manner; then linked fingers for a wish, and could neither of them think of one.

By the time they had finished, and cleared away, it was half past five. They passed into the hall together.

"You must get some more sleep," said Jim Airth, authoritatively.

"I will, if you wish it," whispered Myra; "but I never, in my whole life, felt so strong or so rested. Jim, I shall sit at your table, and pour out your coffee at breakfast. Let's aim to have it at nine, as usual. It will be such fun to watch the Murgatroyds, and to remember our cheese and beer. If you are down first, order our breakfasts at the same table."

"All right," said Jim Airth.

Myra commenced mounting the stairs, but turned on the fifth step and hung over the banisters to smile at him.

Jim Airth reached up his hand. "How can I let you go?" he exclaimed suddenly.

Myra leaned over, and smiled into his adoring eyes.

"How can I go?" she whispered, tenderly.

Jim Airth took both her hands in his. His eyes blazed up into hers.

"Myra," he said, "when shall we be married?"

Myra's face flamed, just as the soft white clouds had flamed when the sun arose. But she met the fire of his eyes without flinching.

"When you will, Jim," she answered gently.

"As soon as possible, then," said Jim Airth, eagerly.

Myra withdrew her hands, and mounted two more steps; then turned to bend and whisper: "Why?"

"Because," replied Jim Airth, "I do not know how to bear that there should be a day, or an hour, or a minute, when we cannot be together."

"Ah, do you feel that, too?" whispered Myra.

"Too?" cried Jim Airth. "Do you—Myra! Come back!"

But Lady Ingleby fled up the stairs like a hare. She had not run so fast since she was a little child of ten. He heard her happy laugh, and the closing of her door.

Then he unbarred the front entrance; and stepping out, stood in the sunshine, on the path where he had seen his Fairy-land Princess arrive.

He stretched his arms over his head.

"Mine!" he said. "Mine, altogether! Oh, my God! At last, I have won the Highest!"

Then he raced down the street to the beach; and five minutes later, in the full strength of his vigorous manhood, he was swimming up the golden path, towards the rising sun.

CHAPTER XIV

GOLDEN DAYS

The week which followed was one of ideal joy and holiday. Both knew, instinctively, that no after days could ever be quite as these first days. They were an experience which came not again, and must be realised and enjoyed with whole-hearted completeness.

At first Jim Airth talked with determination of a special licence, and pleaded for no delay. But Lady Ingleby, usually vague to a degree on all questions of law or matters of business, fortunately felt doubtful as to whether it would be wise to be married in a name other than her own; and, though she might have solved the difficulty by at once revealing her identity to Jim Airth, she was anxious to choose her own time and place for this revelation, and had set her heart upon making it amid the surroundings of her own beautiful home at Shenstone.

"You see, Jim," she urged, "I have a few friends in town and at Shenstone, who take an interest in my doings; and I could hardly reappear among them married! Could I, Jim? It would seem such an unusual and unexpected termination to a rest-cure. Wouldn't it, Jim?"

Jim Airth's big laugh brought Miss Susie to the window. It caused sad waste of Susannah's time, that her window looked out on the honeysuckle arbour.

"It might make quite a run on rest-cures," said Jim Airth.

"Ah, but they couldn't all meet you," said Myra; and the look he received from those sweet eyes, atoned for the vague inaccuracy of the rejoinder.

So they agreed to have one week of this free untrammelled life, before returning to the world of those who knew them; and he promised to come and see her in her own home, before taking the final steps which should make her altogether his.

So they went gay walks along the cliffs in the breezy sunshine; and Myra, clinging to Jim's arm, looked down from above upon their ledge.

They revisited Horseshoe Cove at low water, and Jim Airth spent hours cutting the hurried niches into proper steps, so as to leave a staircase to the ledge, up which people, who chanced in future to be caught by the tide, might climb to safety. Myra sat on the beach and watched him, her eyes alight with tender memories; but she absolutely refused to mount again.

"No, Jim," she said; "not until we come here on our honeymoon. Then, if you wish, you shall take your wife back to the place where we passed those wonderful hours. But not now."

Jim, who expected always to have his own way, unless he was given excellent reasons in black and white for not having it, was about to expostulate and insist, when he saw tears on her lashes and a quiver of the sweet smiling lips, and gave in at once without further question.

They hired a tent, and pitched it on the shore at Tregarth, Myra telegraphed for a bathing-dress, and Jim went into the sea in his flannels and tried to teach her to swim, holding her up beneath her chin and saying; "One, two! ONE, TWO!" far louder than Myra had ever had it said to her before. Thus, amid much splashing and laughter, Lady Ingleby accomplished her swim of ten yards.

Miss Murgatroyd was shocked; nay, more than shocked. Miss Murgatroyd was scandalised! She took to her bed forthwith, expecting Miss Eliza and Miss Susannah to follow her example—in the spirit, if not to the letter. But, released from Amelia's personal supervision, romantic little Susie led Eliza astray; and the two took a furtive and fearful joy in seeing all they could of the "goings on" of the couple who had boldly converted the prosaic Cornish hotel into a land of excitement and romance.

From the moment when on the morning after their adventure, Myra, with yellow roses in the belt of her white gown, had swept into the coffee-room at five minutes past nine, saying: "My dear Jim, have I kept you waiting? I hope the coffee is not cold?"—all life had seemed transformed to Miss Susie. Turning quickly, she had caught the look Jim Airth gave to the lovely woman who took her place opposite him at his hitherto lonely table, and, still smiling into his eyes, lifted the coffee-pot.

Amelia's stern whisper had recalled her to her senses, and prevented any further glancing round; but she had heard Myra say: "I forgot your sugar, Jim. One lump, or two?" and Jim Airth's reply: "As usual, thanks, dear," not knowing, that with a silent twinkle of fun, he laid an envelope over his cup, as a sign to Myra, waiting with poised sugar-tongs, that "as usual" meant no sugar at all!

Later on, when she one day met Lady Ingleby alone in a passage, Miss Susannah ventured two hurried questions.

"Oh, tell me, my dear! Is it really true that you are going to marry Mr. Airth? And have you known him long?"

And Myra smiling down into Susie's plump anxious face replied: "Well, as a matter of fact, Miss Susannah, Jim Airth is going to marry me. And I cannot explain how long I have known him. I seem to have known him all my life."

72

"Ah," whispered Miss Susannah with a knowing smile of conscious perspicacity; "Eliza and I felt sure it was a tiff."

This remark appeared absolutely incomprehensible to Lady Ingleby; and not until she had repeated it to Jim, and he had shouted with laughter, and called her a bare-faced deceiver, did she realise that the "tiff" was supposed to have been operative during the whole time she and Jim Airth had sat at separate tables, and showed no signs of acquaintance.

However, she smiled kindly into the archly nodding face. Then, in the consciousness of her own great happiness, enveloped little Susie in her beautiful arms, and kissed her.

Miss Susannah never forgot that embrace. It was to her a reflected realisation of what it must be to be loved by Jim Airth. And, thereafter, whenever Miss Murgatroyd saw fit to use such adjectives as "indecent," "questionable," or "highly improper," Miss Susie bravely gathered up her wool-work, and left the room.

Thus the golden days went by, and a letter came for Jim Airth from Lady Ingleby's secretary. Her ladyship was away at present but would be returning to Shenstone on the following Monday, and would be pleased to give him an interview on Tuesday afternoon. The two o'clock express from Charing Cross would be met at Shenstone station, unless he wrote suggesting another.

"Now that is very civil," said Jim to Myra, as he passed her the letter, "and how well it suits our plans. We had already arranged both to go up to town on Monday, and you on to Shenstone. So I can come down by that two o'clock train on Tuesday, get my interview with Lady Ingleby over as quickly as may be, and dash off to my girl at the Lodge. I hope to goodness she won't want to give me tea!"

"Which 'she'?" asked Myra, smiling. "I shall certainly want to give you tea."

"Then I shall decline Lady Ingleby's," said Jim with decision.

Even during those wonderful days he went on steadily with his book, Myra sitting near him in the smoking-room, writing letters or reading, while he worked. "I do better work if you are within reach, or at all events, within sight," Jim had said; and it was impossible that Lady Ingleby's mind should not have contrasted the thrill of pleasure this gave her, with the old sense of being in the way if work was to be done; and of being shut out from the chief interests of Michael's life, by the closing of the laboratory door. Ah, how different from the way in which Jim already made her a part of himself, enfolding her into his every interest.

She wrote fully of her happiness to Mrs. Dalmain, telling her in detail the unusual happenings which had brought it so rapidly to pass. Also a few lines to her old friend the Duchess of Meldrum, merely announcing the fact of her engagement and the date of her return to Shenstone, promising full particulars later. This letter held also a message for Ronald and Billy, should they chance to be at Overdene.

Sunday evening, their last at Tregarth, came all too soon. They went to the little church together, sitting among the simple fisher folk at Evensong. As they looked over one hymn book, and sang "Eternal Father, strong to save," both thought of "Davy Jones" in the middle of the hymn, and had to exchange a smile; yet with an instant added reverence of petition and thanksgiving.

> "Thus evermore, shall rise to Thee,
> Glad hymns of praise from land and sea."

Jim Airth's big bass boomed through the little church; and Myra, close to his shoulder, sang with a face so radiant that none could doubt the reality of her praise.

Then back to a cold supper at the Moorhead Inn; after which they strolled out to the honeysuckle arbour for Jim's evening pipe, and a last quiet talk.

It was then that Jim Airth said, suddenly: "By the way I wish you would tell me more about Lady Ingleby. What kind of a woman is she? Easy to talk to?"

For a moment Myra was taken aback. "Why, Jim—I hardly know. Easy? Yes, I think you will find her easy to talk to."

"Does she speak of her husband's death, or is it a tabooed subject?"

"She speaks of it," said Myra, softly, "to those who can understand."

"Ah! Do you suppose she will like to hear details of those last days?"

"Possibly; if you feel inclined to give them, Jim—do you know who did it?"

A surprised silence in the arbour. Jim removed his pipe, and looked at her.

"Do I know—who—did—what?" he asked slowly.

"Do you know the name of the man who made the mistake which killed Lord Ingleby?"

Jim returned his pipe to his mouth.

"Yes, dear, I do," he said, quietly. "But how came you to know of the blunder? I thought the whole thing was hushed up, at home."

"It was," said Myra; "but Lady Ingleby was told, and I heard it then. Jim, if she asked you the name, should you tell her?"

"Certainly I should," replied Jim Airth. "I was strongly

74

opposed, from the first, to any mystery being made about it. I hate a hushing-up policy. But there was the fellow's future to consider. The world never lets a thing of that sort drop. He would always have been pointed out as 'The chap who killed Ingleby'—just as if he had done it on purpose; and every man of us knew that would be a millstone round the neck of any career. And then the whole business had been somewhat irregular; and 'the powers that be' have a way of taking all the kudos, if experiments are successful; and making a what-on-earth-were-you-dreaming-of row, if they chance to be a failure. Hence the fact that we are all such stick-in-the-muds, in the service. Nobody dares be original. The risks are too great, and too astonishingly unequal. If you succeed, you get a D.S.O. from a grateful government, and a laurel crown from an admiring nation. If you fail, an indignant populace derides your name, and a pained and astonished government claps you into jail. That's not the way to encourage progress, or make fellows prompt to take the initiative. The right or the wrong of an action should not be determined by its success or failure."

Lady Ingleby's mind had paused at the beginning of Jim's tirade.

"They could not have taken Michael's kudos," she said. "It must have been patented. He was always most careful to patent all his inventions."

"Eh, what?" said Jim Airth. "Oh, I see. 'Kudos,' my dear girl, means 'glory'; not a new kind of explosive. And why do you call Lord Ingleby 'Michael'?"

"I knew him intimately," said Lady Ingleby.

"I see. Well, as I was saying, I protested about the hushing up, but was talked over; and the few who knew the facts pledged their word of honour to keep silence. Only, the name was to be given to Lady Ingleby, if she desired to know it; and some of us thought you might as well put it in The Times at once, as tell a woman. Then we heard she had decided not to know."

"What do you think of her decision?" asked Lady Ingleby.

"I think it proved her to be a very just-minded woman, and a very unusual one, if she keeps to it. But it would be rather like a woman, to make a fine decision such as that during the tension of a supreme moment, and then indulge in private speculation afterwards."

"Did you hear her reason, Jim? She said she did not wish that a man should walk this earth, whose hand she could not bring herself to touch in friendship."

"Poor loyal soul!" said Jim Airth, greatly moved. "Myra, if I

75

got accidentally done for, as Ingleby was,—should you feel so, for my sake?"

"No!" cried Myra, passionately. "If I lost you, my belovèd, I should never want to touch any other man's hand, in friendship or otherwise, as long as I lived!"

"Ah," mused Jim Airth. "Then you don't consider Lady Ingleby's reason for her decision proved a love such as ours?"

Myra laid her beautiful head against his shoulder.

"Jim," she said, brokenly, "I do not feel myself competent to discuss any other love. One thing only is clear to me;—I never realised what love meant, until I knew you."

A long silence in the honeysuckle arbour.

Then Jim Airth cried almost fiercely to the woman in his arms: "Can you really think you have been right to keep me waiting, even for a day?"

And she who loved him with a love beyond expression could frame no words in answer to that question. Thus it came to pass that, in the days to come, it was there, unanswered; ready to return and beat upon her brain with merciless reiteration: "Was I right to keep him waiting, even for a day."

In the hall, beside the marble table, where lay the visitors' book, they paused to say good-night. From the first, Myra had never allowed him up the stairs until her door was closed. "If you don't keep the rules I think it right to make, Jim," she had said, with her little tender smile, "I shall, in self-defence, engage Miss Murgatroyd as chaperon; and what sort of a time would you have then?"

So Jim was pledged to remain below until her door had been shut five minutes. After which he used to tramp up the stairs whistling:

> "A long long life, to my sweet wife,
> And mates at sea;
> And keep our bones from Davy Jones,
> Where'er we be.
> And may you meet a mate as sweet——"

Then his door would bang, and Myra would venture to give vent to her suppressed laughter, and to sing a soft little

> "Yeo ho! we go!—Yeo ho! Yeo ho!"

for sheer overflowing happiness.

But this was the last evening. A parting impended. Also there had been tense moments in the honeysuckle arbour.

76

Jim's blue eyes were mutinous. He stood holding her hands against his breast, as he had done in Horseshoe Cove, when the waves swept round their feet, and he had cried: "You must climb!"

"So to-morrow night," he said, "you will be at the Lodge, Shenstone; and I, at my Club in town. Do you know how hard it is to be away from you, even for an hour? Do you realise that if you had not been so obstinate we never need have been parted at all? We could have gone away from here, husband and wife together. If you had really cared, you wouldn't have wanted to wait."

Myra smiled up into his angry eyes.

"Jim," she whispered, "it is so silly to say: 'If you had really cared'; because you know, perfectly well, that I care for you, more than any woman in the world has ever cared for any man before! And I do assure you, Jim, that you couldn't have married me validly from here—and think how awful it would be, to love as much as we love and then find out that we were not validly married—and when you come to my home, and fetch me away from there, you will admit—yes really admit—that I was right. You will have to apologise humbly for having said 'Bosh!' so often. Jim—dearest! Look at the clock! I must go. Poor Miss Murgatroyd will grow so tired of listening for us. She always leaves her door a crack open. So does Miss Susannah. They have all taken to sleeping with their doors ajar. I deftly led the conversation round to riddles yesterday, when I was alone with them for a few minutes, and asked sternly: 'When is a door, not a door?' They all answered: 'When it is a jar!' quite unabashed; and Miss Eliza asked another! I believe Susie stands at her crack, in the darkness, in hopes of seeing you march by.... No, don't say naughty words. They are dears, all three of them; and we shall miss them horribly to-morrow. Oh, Jim—I've just had such a brilliant idea! I shall ask them to be my bridesmaids! Can't you see them following me up the aisle? It would be worse than the duchess giving Jane away. Ah, you don't know that story? I will tell it you, some day. Jim, say 'Good-night' quickly, and let me go."

"Once," said Jim Airth, tightening his grasp on her wrists— "once, Myra, we said no 'good-night,' and no 'good-morning.'"

"Jim, darling!" said Myra, gently; "on that night, before I went to sleep, you said to me: 'We are not alone. God is here.' And then you repeated part of the hundred and thirty-ninth psalm. And, Jim—I thought you the best and strongest man I had ever known; and I felt that, all my life, I should trust you, as I trusted my God."

Jim Airth loosed the hands he had held so tightly, and kissed them very gently. "Good-night, my sweetheart," he said, "and God bless you!" Then he turned away to the marble table.

Myra ran swiftly up the stairs and closed her door.

Then she knelt beside her bed, and sobbed uncontrollably; partly for joy, and partly for sorrow. The unanswered question commenced its reiteration: "Ah, was I right to keep him waiting?"

Presently she lifted her head, held her breath, and stared into the darkness. A vision seemed to pass across her room. A tall, bearded man, in evening clothes. In his arms a tiny dog, peeping at her through its curls, as if to say: "I have the better place. Where do you come in?" The tall man turned at the door. "Good-night, my dear Myra," he said, kindly.

The vision passed.

Lady Ingleby buried her face in the bedclothes. "That—for ten long years!" she said. Then, in the darkness, she saw the mutinous fire of Jim Airth's blue eyes, and felt the grip of his strong hands on hers. "How can I say 'Good-night'?" protested his deep voice, passionately. And, with a rush of happy tears, Myra clasped her hands, whispering: "Dear God, am I at last to know the Best?"

And up the stairs came Jim Airth, whistling like a nightingale. But, as a concession to Miss Murgatroyd's ideas concerning suitable Sabbath music, he discarded "Nancy Lee," and whistled:

> "Eternal Father, strong to save,
> Whose arm hath bound the restless wave;
> Who bidst the mighty ocean deep,
> Its own appointed limits keep,
> O hear us, when we cry to Thee——"

And, kneeling beside her bed, in the darkness, Myra made of it her evening prayer.

CHAPTER XV

"WHERE IS LADY INGLEBY?"

When Jim Airth left the train on the following Tuesday afternoon, he looked eagerly up and down the platform, hoping to see Myra. True, they had particularly arranged not to meet, until after his interview with Lady Ingleby. But Myra was so charmingly inconsequent and impulsive in her actions. It would be quite like her to reverse the whole plan they had made; and, if her desire to see him, in any measure resembled his huge hunger for a sight of her, he could easily understand such a reversal.

However, Myra was not there; and with a heavy sense of unreasonable disappointment, Jim Airth chucked his ticket to a waiting porter, passed through the little station, and found a smart turn-out, with tandem ponies, waiting outside.

The groom at the leader's head touched his hat.

"For Shenstone Park, sir?"

"Yes," said Jim Airth, and climbed in.

The groom touched his hat again. "Her ladyship said, sir, that perhaps you might like to drive the ponies yourself, sir."

"No, thank you," said Jim Airth, shortly. "I never drive other people's ponies."

The groom's comprehending grin was immediately suppressed. He touched his hat again; gathered up the reins, mounted the driver's seat, flicked the leader, and the perfectly matched ponies swung at once into a fast trot.

Jim Airth, a connoisseur in horse-flesh, eyed them with approval. They flew along the narrow Surrey lanes, between masses of wild roses and clematis. The villagers were working in the hayfields, shouting gaily to one another as they tossed the hay. It was a matchless June day, in a perfect English summer.

Jim Airth's disappointment at Myra's non-appearance, was lifting rapidly in the enjoyment of the drive. After all it was best to adhere to plans once made; and every step of these jolly little tapping hoofs was bringing him nearer to the Lodge. Perhaps she would be at the window. (He had particularly told her not to be!)

"These ponies have been well handled," he remarked approvingly to the groom, as they flew round a bend.

"Yes, sir," said the groom, with the inevitable movement towards his hat, whip and hand going up together. "Her ladyship always drives them herself, sir. Fine whip, her ladyship, sir."

This item of information surprised Jim Airth. Judging by Lord Ingleby's age and appearance, he had expected to find Lady Ingleby a sedate and stately matron of sixty. It was somewhat surprising to hear of her as a fine whip.

However, he had no time to weigh the matter further. Passing an ivy-clad church on the village green, they swung through massive iron gates, of very fine design, and entered the stately avenue of Shenstone Park. To the left, in a group of trees, stood a pretty little gabled house.

"What house is that?" asked Jim Airth, quickly.

"The Lodge, sir."

"Who lives there?"

"Mrs. O'Mara, sir."

"Has Mrs. O'Mara returned?"

"I don't know, sir. She was up at the house with her ladyship this morning."

"Then she has returned," said Jim Airth.

The groom looked perplexed, but made no comment.

Jim Airth turned in his seat, and looked back at the Lodge. It was a far smaller house than he had expected. This fact did not seem to depress him. He smiled to himself, as at some thought which gave him amusement and pleasure. While he still looked back, a side door opened; a neatly dressed woman in black, apparently a superior lady's-maid, appeared on the doorstep, shook out a white table-cloth, and re-entered the house.

They flew on up the avenue, Jim Airth noting every tree with appreciation and pleasure. The fine old house came into view, and a moment later they drew up at the entrance.

"Good driving," remarked Jim Airth approvingly, as he tipped the little groom. Then he turned, to find the great doors already standing wide, and a stately butler, with immense black eyebrows, waiting to receive him.

"Will you come to her ladyship's sitting-room, sir?" said the butler, and led the way.

Jim Airth entered a charmingly appointed room, and looked around.

It was empty.

"Kindly wait here, sir, while I acquaint her ladyship with your arrival," said the pompous person with the eyebrows, and went out noiselessly, closing the door behind him.

Left alone, Jim Airth commenced taking rapid note of the room, hoping to gain therefrom some ideas as to the tastes and character of its possessor. But almost immediately his attention was arrested by a life-size portrait of Lord Ingleby, hanging above the mantelpiece.

Jim Airth walked over to the hearthrug, and stood long, looking with silent intentness at the picture.

"Excellent," he said to himself, at last. "Extraordinarily clever. That chap shall paint Myra, if I can lay hands on him. What a jolly little dog! And what devotion! Mutual and absorbing. I suppose that is Peter. Queer to think that I should have been the last to hear him calling Peter. I wonder whether Lady Ingleby liked Peter. If not, I doubt if she would have had much of a look-in. If anyone went to the wall it certainly wasn't Peter."

He was still absorbed in the picture, when the butler returned with a long message, solemnly delivered.

"Her ladyship is out in the grounds, sir. As it is so warm in the house, sir, her ladyship requests that you come to her in the grounds. If you will allow me, sir, I will show you the way."

Jim Airth restrained an inclination to say: "Buck up!" and followed the butler along a corridor, down a wide staircase to a lower hall. They stepped out on to a terrace running the full length of the house. Below it, an old-fashioned garden, with box borders, bright flower beds, a fountain in the centre. Beyond this a smooth lawn, sloping down to a beautiful lake, which sparkled and gleamed in the afternoon sunshine. On this lawn, well to the right, half-way between the house and the water, stood a group of beeches. Beneath their spreading boughs, in the cool inviting shadow, were some garden chairs. Jim Airth could just discern, in one of these, the white gown of a woman, holding a scarlet parasol.

The butler indicated this clump of trees.

"Her ladyship said, sir, that she would await you under the beeches."

He returned to the house, and Jim Airth was left to make his way alone to Lady Ingleby, guided by the gleam among the trees of her brilliant parasol. Even at that moment it gave him pleasure to find Lady Ingleby's taste in sunshades, resembling Myra's.

He stood for a minute on the terrace, taking in the matchless beauty of the place. Then his face grew sad and stern. "What a home to leave," he said; "and to leave it, never to return!"

He still wore a look of sadness as he descended the steps leading to the flower garden, made his way along the narrow gravel paths; then stepped on to the soft turf of the lawn, and walked towards the clump of beeches.

Jim Airth—tall and soldierly, broad-shouldered and erect— might have made an excellent impression upon Lady Ingleby, had she watched his coming. But she kept her parasol between herself and her approaching guest.

In fact he drew quite near; near enough to distinguish the ripples of soft lace about, her feet, the long graceful sweep of her gown; and still she seemed unconscious of his close proximity.

He passed beneath the beeches and stood before her. And, even then, the parasol concealed her face.

But Jim Airth was never at a loss, when sure of his ground. "Lady Ingleby," he said, with grave formality; "I was told to——"

Then the parasol was flung aside, and he found himself looking down into the lovely laughing eyes of Myra.

To see Jim Airth's face change from its look of formal gravity to one of rapturous delight, was to Myra well worth the long effort of sitting immovable. He flung himself down before her with boyish abandon, and clasped both herself and her chair in his long arms.

"Oh, you darling!" he said, bending his face over hers, while his blue eyes danced with delight. "Oh, Myra, what centuries since yesterday! How I have longed for you. I almost hoped you would after all have come to the station. How I have grudged wasting all this time in coming to call on old Lady Ingleby. Myra, has it seemed long to you? Do you realise, my dear girl, that it can't go on any longer; that we cannot possibly live through another twenty-four hours of separation? But oh, you Tease! There was I, ramping with impatience at every wasted moment; and here were you, sitting under this tree, hiding your face and pretending to be Lady Ingleby! The astonished and astonishing old party in the eyebrows, certainly pointed you out as Lady Ingleby when he started me off on my pilgrimage. I say, how lovely you look! What billowy softness! It wouldn't do for cliff-climbing; but its A.I. for sitting on lawns.... I can't help it! I must!"

"Jim," said Myra, laughing and pushing him away; "what has come to you, you dearest old boy? You will really have to behave! We are not in the honeysuckle arbour. 'The astonishing old party in the eyebrows' is most likely observing us from a window, and will have good cause to look astonished, if he sees you 'carrying on' in such a manner. Jim, how nice you look in your town clothes. I always like a grey frock-coat. Stand up, and let me see.... Oh, look at the green of the turf on those immaculate knees! What a pity. Did you don all this finery for me?"

"Of course not, silly!" said Jim Airth, rubbing his knees vigorously. "When I haul you up cliffs, I wear old Norfolk coats; and when I duck you in the sea, I wear flannels. I considered this the correct attire in which to pay a formal call on Lady Ingleby; and now, before she has had a chance of being duly impressed by it, I

82

have spoilt my knees hopelessly, worshipping at your shrine! Where is Lady Ingleby? Why doesn't she keep her appointments?"

"Jim," said Myra, looking up at him with eyes full of unspeakable love, yet dancing with excitement and delight; "Jim, do you admire this place?"

"This place?" cried Jim, stepping back a pace, so as to command a good view of the lake and woods beyond. "It is absolutely perfect. We have nothing like this in Scotland. You can't beat for all round beauty a real old mellow lived-in English country seat; especially when you get a twenty acre lake, with islands and swans, all complete. And I suppose the woods beyond, as far as one can see, belong to the Inglebys—or rather, to Lady Ingleby. What a pity there is no son."

"Jim," said Myra, "I have so looked forward to showing you my home."

He stepped close to her at once. "Then show it to me, dear," he said. "I would rather be alone with you in your own little home—I saw it, as we drove up—than waiting about, in this vast expanse of beauty, for Lady Ingleby."

"Jim," said Myra, "do you remember a little tune I often hummed down in Cornwall; and, when you asked me what it was, I said you should hear the words some day?"

Jim looked puzzled. "Really dear—you hummed so many little tunes——"

"Oh, I know," said Myra; "and I have not much ear. But this was very special. I want to sing it to you now. Listen!"

And looking up at him, her soft eyes full of love, Myra sang, with slight alterations of her own, the last verse of the old Scotch ballad, "Huntingtower."

> "Blair in Athol's mine, Jamie,
> Fair Dunkeld is mine, laddie;
> Saint Johnstown's bower,
> And Huntingtower,
> And all that's mine, is thine, laddie."

"Very pretty," said Jim, "but you've mixed it, my dear. Jamie bestowed all his possessions on the lassie. You sang it the wrong way round."

"No, no," cried Myra, eagerly. "There is no wrong way round. Providing they both love, it does not really matter which gives. The one who happens to possess, bestows. If you were a cowboy, Jim, and you loved a woman with lands and houses, in taking her, you would take all that was hers."

"I guess I'd take her out to my ranch and teach her to milk cows," laughed Jim Airth. Then turning about under the tree and looking in all directions: "But seriously, Myra, where is Lady Ingleby? She should keep her appointments. We cannot waste our whole afternoon waiting here. I want my girl; and I want her in her own little home, alone. Cannot we find Lady Ingleby?"

Then Myra rose, radiant, and came and stood before him. The sunbeams shone through the beech leaves and danced in her grey eyes. She had never looked more perfect in her sweet loveliness. The man took it all in, and the glory of possession lighted his handsome face.

She came and stood before him, laying her hands upon his breast. He wrapped his arms lightly about her. He saw she had something to say; and he waited.

"Jim," said Myra, "Jim, dearest. There is just one name I want to bear, more than any other. There is just one thing I long to be. Then I shall be content. I want to have the right to be called 'Mrs. Jim Airth.' I want more than all else beside, to be your wife. But—until I am that; and may it be very soon! until you make me 'Mrs. Jim Airth'—dearest—I—am Lady Ingleby."

84

CHAPTER XVI

UNDER THE BEECHES AT SHENSTONE

Jim Airth's arms fell slowly to his sides. He still looked into those happy, loving eyes, but the joy in his own died out, leaving them merely cold blue steel. His face slowly whitened, hardened, froze into lines of silent misery. Then he moved back a step, and Myra's hands fell from him.

"You—'Lady Ingleby'?" he said.

Myra gazed at him, in unspeakable dismay.

"Jim!" she cried, "Jim, dearest! Why should you mind it so much?"

She moved forward, and tried to take his hand.

"Don't touch me!" he said, sharply. Then: "You, Myra? You! Lord Ingleby's widow?"

The furious misery of his voice stung Myra. Why should he resent the noble name she bore, the high rank which was hers? Even if it placed her socially far above him, had she not just expressed her readiness—her longing—to resign all, for him? Had not her love already placed him on the topmost pinnacle of her regard? Was it generous, was it worthy of Jim Airth to take her disclosure thus?

She moved towards the chairs, with gentle dignity.

"Let us sit down, Jim, and talk it over," she said, quietly. "I do not think you need find it so overwhelming a matter as you seem to imagine. Let me tell you all about it; or rather, suppose you ask me any questions you like."

Jim Airth sat blindly down upon the chair farthest from her, put his elbows on his knees, and sank his face into his hands.

Without any comment, Myra rose; moved her chair close enough to enable her to lay her hand upon his arm, should she wish to do so; sat down again, and waited in silence.

Jim Airth had but one question to ask. He asked it, without lifting his head.

"Who is Mrs. O'Mara?"

"She is the widow of Sergeant O'Mara who fell at Targai. We both lost our husbands in that disaster, Jim. She had been for many years my maid-attendant. When she married the sergeant, a fine soldier whom Michael held in high esteem, I wished still to keep her near me. Michael had given me the Lodge to do with as I pleased. I put them into it. She lives there still. Oh, Jim dearest, try to realise that I have not said one word to you which was not completely truthful! Let me explain how I came to be in Cornwall under her name instead of my own. If I might put my hand in yours, Jim, I could tell you more easily.... No? Very well; never mind.

"After I received the telegram last November telling me of my husband's death, I had a very bad nervous breakdown. I do not think it was caused so much by my loss, as by a prolonged mental strain, which had preceded it. Just as I had moved to town and was getting better, full details arrived, and I had to be told that it had been an accident. You know all about the question as to whether I should hear the name or not. You also know my decision. The worry of this threw me back. What you said in the arbour was perfectly true. I am a woman, Jim; often, a weak one; and I was very much alone. I decided rightly, in a supreme moment—possibly you may know who it was who graciously undertook to bring me the news from the War Office—but, afterwards, I began to wonder; I allowed myself to guess. Men from the front came home. My surmisings circled ceaselessly around two—dear fellows, of whom I was really fond. At last I felt convinced I knew, by intangible yet unmistakable signs, which was he who had done it. I grew quite sure. And then—I hardly know how to tell you, Jim—of all impossible horrors! The man who had killed Michael wanted to marry me!—Oh, don't groan, darling; you make me so unhappy! But I do not wonder you find it difficult to believe. He cared very much, poor boy; and I suppose he thought that, as I should remain in ignorance, the fact need not matter. It seems hard to understand; but a man in love sometimes loses all sense of proportion—at least so I once heard someone say; or words to that effect. I did not allow it ever to reach the point of an actual proposal; but I felt I must flee away. There were others—and it was terrible to me. I loved none of them; and I had made up my mind never to marry again unless I found my ideal. Oh, Jim!"

She laid her hand upon his knee. It might have been a falling leaf, for all the sign he gave. She left it there, and went on speaking.

"People gossiped. Society papers contained constant trying paragraphs. Even my widow's weeds were sketched and copied. My nerves grew worse. Life seemed unendurable.

"At last I consulted a great specialist, who is also a trusted friend. He ordered me a rest-cure. Not to be shut up within four walls with my own worries, but to go right away alone; to leave my own identity, and all appertaining thereto, completely behind; to go to a place to which I had never before been, where I knew no one, and should not be known; to live in the open air; fare simply; rise early, retire early; but, above all, as he quaintly said: 'Leave Lady Ingleby behind.'

"I followed his advice to the letter. He is not a man one can disobey. I did not like the idea of taking a fictitious name, so I decided to be 'Mrs. O'Mara,' and naturally entered her address in the visitors' book, as well as her name.

"Oh, that evening of arrival! You were quite right, Jim. I felt just a happy child, entering a new world of beauty and delight—all holiday and rest.

"And then—I saw you! And, oh my belovèd, I think almost from the first moment my soul flew to you, as to its unquestioned mate! Your vitality became my source of vigour; your strength filled and upheld everything in me which had been weak and faltering. I owed you much, before we had really spoken. Afterwards, I owed you life itself, and love, and all—ALL, Jim!"

Myra paused, silently controlling her emotion; then, bending forward, laid her lips upon the roughness of his hair. It might have been the stirring of the breeze, for all the sign he made.

"When I found at first that you had come from the war, when I realised that you must have known Michael, I praised the doctor's wisdom in making me drop my own name. Also the Murgatroyds would have known it immediately, and I should have had no peace, As it was, Miss Murgatroyd occasionally held forth in the sitting-room concerning 'poor dear Lady Ingleby,' whom she gave us to understand she knew intimately. And then—oh, Jim! when I came to know my cosmopolitan cowboy; when he told me he hated titles and all that appertained to them; then indeed I blessed the moment when I had writ myself down plain 'Mrs. O'Mara'; and I resolved not to tell him of my title until he loved me enough not to mind it, or wanted me enough, to change me at once from Lady Ingleby of Shenstone Park, into plain Mrs. Jim Airth of—anywhere he chooses to take me!

"Now you will understand why I felt I could not marry you validly in Cornwall; and I wanted—was it selfish?—I wanted the joy of revealing my own identity when I had you, at last, in my own beautiful home. Oh, my dear—my dear! Cannot our love stand the test of so light a thing as this?"

She ceased speaking and waited.

She was sure of her victory; but it seemed strange, in dealing with so fine a nature as that of the man she loved, that she should have had to fight so hard over what appeared to her a paltry matter. But she knew false pride often rose gigantic about the smallest things; the very unworthiness of the cause seeming to add to the unreasonable growth of its dimensions.

She was deeply hurt; but she was a woman, and she loved him. She waited patiently to see his love for her arise victorious over unworthy pride.

At last Jim Airth stood up.

"I cannot face it yet," he said, slowly. "I must be alone. I ought to have known from the very first that you were—are—Lady Ingleby. I am very sorry that you should have to suffer for that which is no fault of your own. I must—go—now. In twenty-four hours, I will come back to talk it over."

He turned, without another word; without a touch; without a look. He swung round on his heel, and walked away across the lawn.

Myra's dismayed eyes could scarcely follow him.

He mounted the terrace; passed into the house. A door closed.

Jim Airth was gone!

CHAPTER XVII

"SURELY YOU KNEW?"

Myra Ingleby rose and wended her way slowly towards the house.

A stranger meeting her would probably have noticed nothing amiss with the tall graceful woman, whose pallor might well have been due to the unusual warmth of the day.

But the heart within her was dying.

Her joy had received a mortal wound. The man she adored, with a love which had placed him at the highest, was slowly slipping from his pedestal, and her hands were powerless to keep him there.

A woman may drag her own pride in the dust, and survive the process; but when the man she loves falls, then indeed her heart dies within her.

She had loved to call Jim Airth a cowboy. She knew him to be avowedly cosmopolitan. But was he also a slave to vulgar pride? Being plain Jim Airth himself, did he grudge noble birth and ancient lineage to those to whom they rightfully belonged? Professing to scorn titles, did he really set upon them so exaggerated a value, that he would turn from the woman he was about to wed, merely because she owned a title, while he had none?

Myra, entering the house, passed to her sitting-room. Green awnings shaded the windows. The fireplace was banked with ferns and lilies. Bowls of roses stood about; while here and there pots of growing freesias poured their delicate fragrance around.

Myra crossed to the hearthrug and stood gazing up at the picture of Lord Ingleby. The gentle refinement of the scholarly face seemed accentuated by the dim light. Lady Ingleby dwelt in memory upon the consistent courtesy of the dead man's manner; his unfailing friendliness and equability to all; courteous to men of higher rank, considerate to those of lower; genial to rich and poor alike.

"Oh, Michael," she whispered, "have I been unfaithful? Have I forgotten how good you were?"

But still her heart died within her. The man who had stalked across the lawn, leaving her without a touch or look, held it in the hollow of his hand.

A dog-cart clattered up to the portico. Men's voices sounded in the hall. Tramping feet hurried along the corridor. Then Billy's excited young voice cried, "May we come in?" followed by Ronnie's deeper tones, "If we shall not be in the way?" The next moment she was grasping a hand of each.

"You dear boys!" she said. "I have never been more glad to see you! Do sit down; or have you come to play tennis?"

"We have come to see you, dear Queen," said Billy. "We are staying at Overdene. The duchess had your letter. She told us the great news; also, that you were returning yesterday. So we came over to—to——"

"To congratulate," said Ronald Ingram; and he said it heartily and bravely.

"Thank you," said Myra, smiling at them, but her sweet voice was tremulous. These first congratulations, coming just now, were almost more than she could bear. Then, with characteristic simplicity and straightforwardness, she told these old friends the truth.

"You dear boys! It is quite sweet of you to come over; and an hour ago, you would have found me radiant. There cannot have been a happier woman in the whole world than I. But, you know, I met him, and we became engaged, while I was doing my very original rest-cure, which consisted chiefly in being Mrs. O'Mara, to all intents and purposes, instead of myself. This afternoon he knows for the first time that I am Lady Ingleby of Shenstone. And, boys, the shock has been too much for him. He is such a splendid man; but a dear delightful cowboy sort of person. He has lived a great deal abroad, and been everything you can imagine that bestrides a horse and does brave things. He finished up at your horrid little war, and got fever at Targai. You must have known him. He calls it 'a muddle on the frontier,' and now he is writing a book about it, and about other muddles, and how to avoid them. But he has a quite eccentric dislike to titles and big properties; so he has shied really badly at mine. He has gone off to 'face it out' alone. Hence you find me sad instead of gay."

Billy looked at Ronnie, telegraphing: "Is it? It must be! Shall we tell her?"

Ronnie telegraphed back: "It is! It can be no other. You tell her."

Lady Ingleby became aware of these crosscurrents.

"What is it, boys?" she said,

"Dear Queen," cried Billy, with hardly suppressed excitement; "may we ask the cowboy person's name?"

"Jim Airth," replied Lady Ingleby, a sudden rush of colour flooding her pale cheeks.

"In that case," said Billy, "he is the chap we met tearing along to the railway station, as if all the furies were loose at his heels. He looked neither to the right nor to the left, nor, for that matter, in front of him; and our dog-cart had to take to the path! So he did not see two old comrades, nor did he hear their hail. But he cannot possibly have been fleeing from your title, dear lady, and hardly from your property; seeing that his own title is about the oldest known in Scottish history; while mile after mile of moor and stream and forest belong to him. Surely you knew that the fellow who called himself 'Jim Airth' when out ranching in the West, and still keeps it as his nom-de-plume, is—when at home—James, Earl of Airth and Monteith, and a few other names I have forgotten;—the finest old title in Scotland!"

CHAPTER XVIII

WHAT BILLY HAD TO TELL

"Did you bring your rackets, boys?" Lady Ingleby had said, with fine self-control; adding, when they admitted rackets left in the hall, "Ah, I am glad you never can resist the chestnut court. It seems ages since I saw you two fight out a single. Do go on and begin. I will order tea out there in half an hour, and follow you."

Then she escaped to the terrace, flew across garden and lawn, and sought the shelter of the beeches. Arrived there, she sank into the chair in which Jim Airth had sat so immovable, and covered her face with her trembling fingers.

"Oh, Jim, Jim!" she sobbed. "My darling, how grievously I wronged you! My king among men! How I misjudged you! Imputing to you thoughts of which you, in your noble large-heartedness, would scarcely know the meaning. Oh, my dear, forgive me! And oh, come to me through this darkness and explain what I have done wrong; explain what it is you have to face; tell me what has come between us. For indeed, if you leave me, I shall die."

Myra now felt certain that the fault was hers; and she suffered less than when she had thought it his. Yet she was sorely perplexed. For, if the Earl of Airth and Monteith might write himself down "Jim Airth" in the Moorhead Inn visitors' book, and be blameless, why might not Lady Ingleby of Shenstone take an equally simple name, without committing an unpardonable offence?

Myra pondered, wept, and reasoned round in a circle, growing more and more bewildered and perplexed.

But by-and-by she went indoors and tried to remove all traces of recent tears. She must not let her sorrow make her selfish. Ronald and Billy would be wanting tea, and expecting her to join them.

Meanwhile the two friends, their rackets under their arms, had strolled through the shrubbery at the front of the house, to the beautiful tennis lawns, long renowned as being the most perfect in the neighbourhood. Many a tournament had there been fought out, in presence of a gay crowd, lining the courts, beneath the shady chestnut trees.

But on this day the place seemed sad and deserted. They played one set, in silence, hardly troubling to score; then walked to the net and stood close together, one on either side.

"We must tell her," said Ronald, examining his racket, minutely.

"I suppose we must," agreed Billy, reluctantly. "We could not let her marry him."

"Duffer! you don't suppose he would dream of marrying her? He will come back, and tell her himself to-morrow. We must tell her, to spare her that interview. She need never see him again."

"I say, Ron! Did you see her go quite pink when she told us his name? And in spite of the trouble to-day, she looks half a dozen years younger than when she went away. You know she does, old man!"

"Oh, that's the rest-cure," explained Ronnie, but without much conviction. "Rest-cures always have that effect. That's why women go in for them. Did you ever hear of a man doing a rest-cure?"

"Well, I've heard of you, at Overdene," said Billy, maliciously.

"Rot! You don't call staying with the duchess a rest-cure? Good heavens, man! You get about the liveliest time of your life when her Grace of Meldrum undertakes to nurse you. Did you hear about old Pilberry the parson, and the toucan?"

"Yes, shut up. You've told me that unholy story twice already. I say, Ronnie! We are begging the question. Who's to tell her?"

"You," said Ronald decidedly. "She cares for you like a mother, and will take it more easily from you. Then I can step in, later on, with—er—manly comfort."

"Confound you!" said Billy, highly indignant. "I'm not such a kid as you make out. But I'll tell you this:—If I thought it would be for her real happiness, and could be pulled through, I would tell her I did it; then find Airth to-morrow and tell him I had told her so."

"Ass!" said Ronnie, affectionately. "As if that could mend matters. Don't you know the earl? He was against the hushing-up business from the first. He would simply punch your head for daring to lie to her, and go and tell her the exact truth himself. Besides, at this moment, he is thinking more of his side of the question, than of hers. We fellows have a way of doing that. If he had thought first of her, he would have stayed with her and seen her through, instead of rushing off like this, leaving her heart-broken and perplexed."

"Confound him!" said Billy, earnestly.

"I say, Billy! You know women." It was the first time Ronnie had admitted this. "Don't you think—if a woman turned in horror from a man she had loved, she might—if he were tactfully on the spot—turn to a man who had long loved her, and of whom she had undoubtedly been fond?"

93

"My knowledge of women," declaimed Billy, dramatically, "leads me to hope that she would fall into the arms of the man who loved her well enough to risk incurring her displeasure by bravely telling her himself that which she ought——"

"Confound you!" whispered Ronnie, who had glanced past Billy, "Shut up!—The meshes of this net are better than the other, and the new patent sockets undoubtedly keep it——"

"You patient people!" said Lady Ingleby's voice, just behind Billy. "Don't you badly need tea?"

"We were admiring the new net," said Ronald Ingram, frowning at Billy, who with his back to Lady Ingleby, continued admiring the new net, helplessly speechless!

There were brave attempts at merriment during tea. Ronald told all the latest Overdene stories; then described the annual concert which had just taken place.

"Mrs. Dalmain was there, and sang divinely. She sings her husband's songs; he accompanies her. It is awfully fine to see the light on his blind face as he listens, while her glorious voice comes pouring forth. When the song is over, he gets up from the piano, gives her his arm, and apparently leads her off. Very few people realise that, as a matter of fact, she is guiding him. She gave, as an encore, a jolly little new thing of his—quite simple—but everybody wanted it twice over; an air like summer wind blowing through a pine wood, with an accompaniment like a blackbird whistling; words something about 'On God's fair earth, 'mid blossoms blue'—I forget the rest. Go ahead, Bill!"

> "There is no room for sad despair,
> When heaven's love is everywhere."

quoted Billy, who had an excellent memory.

Myra rose, hastily. "I must go in," she said. "But play as long as you like."

Billy walked beside her towards the shrubbery. "May I come in and see you, presently, dear Queen? There is something I want to say."

"Come when you will, Billy-boy," said Lady Ingleby, with a smile. "You will find me in my sitting-room."

And Billy looked furtively at Ronald, hoping he had not seen. Words and smile undoubtedly partook of the maternal!

It was a very grave-faced young man who, half an hour later, appeared in Lady Ingleby's sitting-room, closing the door carefully behind him. Lady Ingleby knew at once that he had come on some matter which, at all events to himself, appeared of paramount

94

importance. Billy's days of youthful escapades were over. This must be something more serious.

She rose from her davenport and came to the sofa. "Sit down, Billy," she said, indicating an armchair opposite—Lord Ingleby's chair, and little Peter's. Both had now left it empty. Billy filled it readily, unconscious of its associations.

"Rippin' flowers," remarked Billy, looking round the room.

"Yes," said Lady Ingleby. She devoutly hoped Billy was not going to propose.

"Jolly room," said Billy; "at least, I always think so."

"Yes," said Lady Ingleby. "So do I."

Billy's eyes, roaming anxiously around for fresh inspiration, lighted on the portrait over the mantelpiece. He started and paled. Then he knew his hour had come. There must be no more beating about the bush.

Billy was a soldier, and a brave one. He had led a charge once, running up a hill ahead of his men, in face of a perfect hail of bullets. First came Billy; then the battalion. Not a man could keep within fifty yards of him. They always said afterwards that Billy came through that charge alive, because he sprinted so fast, that no bullets could touch him. He rushed at the subject now, with the same headlong courage.

"Lady Ingleby," he said, "there is something Ronnie and I both think you ought to know."

"Is there, Billy?" said Myra. "Then suppose you tell it me."

"We have sworn not to tell," continued Billy; "but I don't care a damn—I mean a pin—for an oath, if your happiness is at stake."

"You must not break an oath, Billy, even for my sake," said Myra, gently.

"Well, you see—if you wished it, you were to be the one exception."

Suddenly Lady Ingleby understood. "Oh, Billy!" she said. "Does Ronald wish me to be told?"

This gave Billy a pang. So Ronnie really counted after all, and would walk in—over the broken hearts of Billy and another—in rôle of manly comforter. It was hard; but, loyally, Billy made answer.

"Yes; Ronnie says it is only right; and I think so too. I've come to do it, if you will let me."

Lady Ingleby sat, with clasped hands, considering. After all, what did it matter? What did anything matter, compared to the trouble with Jim?

She looked up at the portrait; but Michael's pictured face, intent on little Peter, gave her no sign.

If these boys wished to tell her, and get it off their minds, why

95

should she not know? It would put a stop, once for all, to Ronnie's tragic love-making.

"Yes, Billy," she said. "You may as well tell me."

The room was very still. A rosebud tapped twice against the window-pane. It might have been a warning finger. Neither noticed it. It tapped a third time.

Billy cleared his throat, and swallowed, quickly.

Then he spoke.

"The man who made the blunder," he said, "and fired the mine too soon; the man who killed Lord Ingleby, by mistake, was the chap you call 'Jim Airth.'"

CHAPTER XIX

JIM AIRTH DECIDES

Lady Ingleby awaited Jim Airth's arrival, in her sitting-room.

As the hour drew near, she rang the bell.

"Groatley," she said, when the butler appeared, "the Earl of Airth, who was here yesterday, will call again, this afternoon. When his lordship comes, you can show him in here. I shall not be at home to any one else. You need not bring tea until I ring for it."

Then she sat down, quietly waiting.

She had resumed the mourning, temporarily laid aside. The black gown, hanging about her in soft trailing folds, added to the graceful height of her slight figure. The white tokens of widowhood at neck and wrists gave to her unusual beauty a pathetic suggestion of wistful loneliness. Her face was very pale; a purple tint beneath the tired eyes betokened tears and sleeplessness. But the calm steadfast look in those sweet eyes revealed a mind free of all doubt; a heart, completely at rest.

She leaned back among the sofa cushions, her hands folded in her lap, and waited.

Bees hummed in and out of the open windows. The scent of freesias filled the room, delicate, piercingly sweet, yet not oppressive. To one man forever afterwards the scent of freesias recalled that afternoon; the exquisite sweetness of that lovely face; the trailing softness of her widow's gown.

Steps in the hall.

The door opened. Groatley's voice, pompously sonorous, broke into the waiting silence.

"The Earl of Airth, m'lady"; and Jim Airth walked in.

As the door closed behind him, Myra rose.

They stood, silently confronting one another beneath Lord Ingleby's picture.

It almost seemed as though the thoughtful scholarly face must turn from its absorbed contemplation of the little dog, to look down for a moment upon them. They presented a psychological problem—these brave hearts in torment—which would surely have proved interesting to the calm student of metaphysics.

Silently they faced one another for the space of a dozen heart-beats.

Then Myra, with a swift movement, went up to Jim Airth, put her arms about his neck, and laid her head upon his breast.

"I know, my belovèd," she said. "You need not give yourself the pain of trying to tell me."

"How?" A single syllable seemed the most Jim's lips, for the moment, could manage.

"Billy told me. He and Ronald Ingram came over yesterday afternoon, soon after you left. They had passed you, on your way to the station. They thought I ought to know. So Billy told me."

Jim Airth's arms closed round her, holding her tightly.

"My—poor—girl!" he said, brokenly.

"They meant well, Jim. They are dear boys. They knew you would come back and tell me yourself; and they wanted to spare us both that pain. I am glad they did it. You were quite right when you said it had to be faced alone. I could not have been ready for your return, if I had not heard the truth, and had time to face it alone. I am ready now, Jim."

Jim Airth laid his cheek against her soft hair, with a groan.

"I have come to say good-bye, Myra. It is all that remains to be said."

"Good-bye?" Myra raised a face of terrified questioning.

Jim Airth pressed it back to its hiding-place upon his breast.

"I am the man, Myra, whose hand you could never bring yourself to touch in friendship."

Myra lifted her head again. The look in her eyes was that of a woman prepared to fight for happiness and life.

"You are the man," she said, "whose little finger is dearer to me than the whole body of any one else has ever been. Do you suppose I will give you up, Jim, because of a thing which happened accidentally in the past, before you and I had ever met? Ah, how little you men understand a woman's heart! Shall I tell you what I felt when Billy told me, after the first bewildering shock was over? First: sorrow for you, my dearest; a realisation of how appalling the mental anguish must have been, at the time. Secondly: thankfulness—yes, intense overwhelming thankfulness—to know at last what had come between us; and to know it was this thing—this mere ghost out of the past—nothing tangible or real; no wrong of mine against you, or of yours against me; nothing which need divide us."

Jim Airth slowly unlocked his arms, took her by the wrists, holding her hands against his breast. Then he looked into her eyes with a silent sadness, more forcible than speech.

"My own poor girl," he said, at length; "it is impossible for me to marry Lord Ingleby's widow."

The strength of his will mastered hers; and, just as in Horseshoe Cove her fears had yielded to his dauntless courage, so now Myra felt her confidence ebbing away before his stern resolve. Fearful of losing it altogether, she drew away her hands, and turned to the sofa.

"Oh, Jim," she said, "sit down and let us talk it over."

She sank back among the cushions and drawing a bowl of roses hastily toward her, buried her face in them, fearing again to meet the settled sadness of his eyes.

Jim Airth sat down—in the chair left vacant by Lord Ingleby and Peter.

"Listen, dear," he said. "I need not ask you never to doubt my love. That would be absurd from me to you. I love you as I did not know it was possible for a man to love a woman. I love you in such a way that every fibre of my being will hunger for you night and day—through all the years to come. But—well, it would always have come hard to me to stand in another man's shoes, and take what had been his. I did not feel this when I thought I was following Sergeant O'Mara, because I knew he must always have been in all things so utterly apart from you. I could, under different circumstances, have brought myself to follow Ingleby, because I realise that he never awakened in you such love as is yours for me. His possessions would not have weighted me, because it so happens I have lands and houses of my own, where we could have lived. But, to stand in a dead man's shoes, when he is dead through an act of mine; to take to myself another man's widow, when she would still, but for a reckless movement of my own right hand, have been a wife—Myra, I could not do it! Even with our great love, it would not mean happiness. Think of it—think! As we stood together in the sight of God, while the Church, in solemn voice, required and charged us both, as we should answer at the dreadful day of judgment when the secrets of all hearts should be disclosed, that if either of us knew any impediment why we might not be lawfully joined together in matrimony, we should then confess it—I should cry: 'Her husband died by my hand!' and leave the church, with the brand of Cain, and the infamy of David, upon me."

Myra lifted frightened eyes; met his, beseechingly; then bent again over the roses.

"Or, even if I passed through that ordeal, standing mute in the solemn silence, what of the moment when the Church bade me take your right hand in my right hand—Myra, my right hand?"

She rose, came swiftly over, and knelt before him. She took his hand, and covered it with tears and kisses. She held it, sobbing, to her heart.

"Dearest," she said, "I will never ask you to do, for my sake, anything you feel impossible or wrong. But, oh, in this, I know you are mistaken. I cannot argue or explain. I cannot put my reasons into words. But I know our living, longing, love ought to come before the happenings of a dead past. Michael lost his life through an accident. That the accident was caused by a mistake on your part, is fearfully hard for you. But there is no moral wrong in it. You might as well blame the company whose boat took him abroad; or the government which decided on the expedition; or the War Office people, who accepted him when he volunteered. I am sure I don't know what David did; I thought he was a quite excellent person. But I do know about Cain; and I am perfectly certain that the brand of Cain could never rest on anyone, because of an unpremeditated accident. Oh, Jim! Cannot you look at it reasonably?"

"I looked at it reasonably—after a while—until yesterday," said Jim Airth. "At first, of course, all was blank, ghastly despair. Oh, Myra, let me tell you! I have never been able to tell anyone. Go back to the couch; I can't let you kneel here. Sit down over there, and let me tell you."

Lady Ingleby rose at once and returned to her seat; then sat listening—her yearning eyes fixed upon his bowed head. He had momentarily forgotten what the events of that night had cost her; so also had she. Her only thought was of his pain.

Jim Airth began to speak, in low, hurried tones; haunted with a horror of reminiscence.

"I can see it now. The little stuffy tent; the hidden light. I was already sickening for fever, working with a temperature of . I hadn't slept for two nights, and my head felt as if it were two large eyes, and those eyes, both bruises. I knew I ought to knock under and give the job to another man; but Ingleby and I had worked it all out together, and I was dead keen on it. It was a place where no big guns could go; but our little arrangement which you could carry in one hand, would do better and surer work, than half a dozen big guns.

"There was a long wait after Ingleby and the other fellow—it was Ingram—started. Cathcart, left behind with me, was in and out of the tent; but he couldn't stay still two minutes; he was afraid of missing the rush. So I was alone when the signal came. We found afterwards that Ingram had crawled out of the tunnel, and gone to take a message to the nearest ambush. Ingleby was left alone. He signalled: 'Placed,' as agreed. I took it to be 'Fire!' and acted instantly. The moment I had done it, I realised my mistake. But that same instant came the roar, and the hot silent night was turned to pandemonium. I dashed out of the tent, shouting for Ingleby. Good God! It was like hell! The yelling swearing Tommies, making up for the long enforced silence and inaction; the hordes of dark devilish faces, leering in their fury, and jeering at our discomfiture; for

100

inside their outer wall, was a rampart of double the strength, and we were no nearer taking Targai.

"Afterwards—if I hadn't owned up at once to my mistake, nobody would have known how the thing had happened. Even then, they tried to persuade me the wrong signal had been given; but I knew better. And on the spot, it was impossible to find—well, any actual proofs of what had happened. The gap had been filled at once with crowds of yelling jostling Tommies, mad to get into the town. Jove, how those chaps fight when they get the chance. When all was over, several were missing who were not among the dead. They must have forced themselves in where they could not get back, and been taken prisoners. God alone knows their fate, poor beggars. Yet I envied them; for when the row was over, my hell began.

"Myra, I would have given my whole life to have had that minute over again. And it was maddening to know that the business might have been done all right with any old fuse. Only we were so keen over our new ideas for signalling, and our portable electric apparatus. Oh, good Lord! I knew despair, those days and nights! I was down with fever, and they took away my sword, and guns, and razors. I couldn't imagine why. Even despair doesn't take me that way. But if a chap could have come into my tent and said: 'You didn't kill Ingleby after all. He's all right and alive!' I would have given my life gladly for that moment's relief. But no present anguish can undo a past mistake.

"Well, I pulled through the fever; life had to be lived, and I suppose I'm not the sort of chap to take a morbid view. When I found the thing was to be kept quiet; when the few who knew the ins-and-outs stood by me like the good fellows they were, saying it might have happened to any of them, and as soon as I got fit again I should see the only rotten thing would be to let it spoil my future; I made up my mind to put it clean away, and live it down. You know they say, out in the great western country: 'God Almighty hates a quitter.' It is one of the stimulating tenets of their fine practical theology. I had fought through other hard times. I determined to fight through this. I succeeded so well, that it even seemed natural to go on with the work Ingleby and I had been doing together, and carry it through. And when notes of his were needed, I came to his own home without a qualm, to ask his widow—the woman I, by my mistake, had widowed—for permission to have and to use them.

"I came—my mind full of the rich joy of life and love, with scarcely room for a passing pang of regret, as I entered the house without a master, the home without a head, knowing I was about to meet the woman I had widowed. Truly 'The mills of God grind slowly, but they grind exceeding small.' I had thrown off too easily what should have been a lifelong burden of regret.

"In the woman I had widowed I found—the woman I was about to wed! Good God! Was there ever so hard a retribution?"

"Jim," said Myra, gently, "is there not another side to the picture? Does it not strike you that it should have seemed beautiful to find that God in His wonderful providence had put you in a position to be able to take care of Michael's widow, left so helpless and alone; that in saving her life by the strength of your right hand, you had atoned for the death that hand had unwittingly dealt; that, though the past cannot be undone, it can sometimes be wiped out by the present? Oh, Jim! Cannot you see it thus, and keep and hold the right to take care of me forever? My belovèd! Let us never, from this moment, part. I will come away with you at once. We can get a special licence, and be married immediately. We will let Shenstone, and let the house in Park Lane, and live abroad, anywhere you will, Jim; only together—together! Take me away to-day. Maggie O'Mara can attend me, until we are married. But I can't face life without you. Jim—I can't! God knows, I can't!"

Jim Airth looked up, a gleam of hope in his sad eyes.

Then he looked away, that her appealing loveliness might not too much tempt him, while making his decision. He lifted his eyes; and, alas! they fell on the portrait over the mantelpiece.

He shivered.

"I can never marry Lord Ingleby's widow," he said. "Myra, how can you wish it? The thing would haunt us! It would be evil—unnatural. Night and day, it would be there. It would come between us. Some day you would reproach me——"

"Ah, hush!" cried Myra, sharply. "Not that! I am suffering enough. At least spare me that!" Then, putting aside once more her own pain: "Would it not be happiness to you, Jim?" she asked, with wistful gentleness.

"Happiness?" cried Jim Airth, violently, "It would be hell!"

Lady Ingleby rose, her face as white as the large arum lily in the corner behind her.

"Then that settles it," she said; "and, do you know, I think we had better not speak of it any more. I am going to ring for tea. And, if you will excuse me for a few moments, while they are bringing it, I will search among my husband's papers, and try to find those you require for your book."

She passed swiftly out. Through the closed door, the man she left alone heard her giving quiet orders in the hall.

He crossed the room, in two great strides, to follow her. But at the door he paused; turned, and came slowly back.

He stood on the hearthrug, with bent head; rigid, motionless.

Suddenly he lifted his eyes to Lord Ingleby's portrait.

"Curse you!" he said through clenched teeth, and beat his fists upon the marble mantelpiece. "Curse your explosives! And curse your inventions! And curse you for taking her first!" Then he dropped into a chair, and buried his face in his hands. "Oh, God forgive me!" he whispered, brokenly. "But there is a limit to what a man can bear."

He scarcely noticed the entrance of the footman who brought tea. But when a lighter step paused at the door, he lifted a haggard face, expecting to see Myra.

A quiet woman entered, simply dressed in black merino. Her white linen collar and cuffs gave her the look of a hospital nurse. Her dark hair, neatly parted, was smoothly coiled around her head. She came in, deferentially; yet with a quiet dignity of manner.

"I have come to pour your tea, my lord," she said. "Lady Ingleby is not well, and fears she must remain in her room. She asks me to give you these papers."

Then the Earl of Airth and Monteith rose to his feet, and held out his hand.

"I think you must be Mrs. O'Mara," he said. "I am glad to meet you, and it is kind of you to give me tea. I have heard of you before; and I believe I saw you yesterday, on the steps of your pretty house, as I drove up the avenue. Will you allow me to tell you how often, when we stood shoulder to shoulder in times of difficulty and danger, I had reason to respect and admire the brave comrade I knew as Sergeant O'Mara?"

Before quitting Shenstone, Jim Airth sat at Myra's davenport and wrote a letter, leaving it with Mrs. O'Mara to place in Lady Ingleby's hands as soon as he had gone.

"I do not wonder you felt unable to see me again. Forgive me for all the grief I have caused, and am causing, you. I shall go abroad as soon as may be; but am obliged to remain in town until I have completed work which I am under contract with my publishers to finish. It will take a month, at most.

"If you want me, Myra—I mean if you need me—I could come at any moment. A wire to my Club would always find me.

> "May I know how you are?
> "Wholly yours,
> "Jim Airth."

To this Lady Ingleby replied on the following day.
"Dear Jim,

"I shall always want you; but I could never send unless the coming would mean happiness for you.

"I know you decided as you felt right,

"I am quite well.

"God bless you always.

"Myra."

CHAPTER XX

A BETTER POINT OF VIEW

In the days which followed, Jim Airth suffered all the pangs which come to a man who has made a decision prompted by pride rather than by conviction.

It had always seemed to him essential that a man should appear in all things without shame or blame in the eyes of the woman he loved. Therefore, to be obliged suddenly to admit that a fatal blunder of his own had been the cause, even in the past, of irreparable loss and sorrow to her, had been an unacknowledged but intolerable humiliation. That she should have anything to overlook or to forgive in accepting himself and his love, was a condition of things to which he could not bring himself to submit; and her sweet generosity and devotion, rather increased than soothed his sense of wounded pride.

He had been superficially honest in the reasons he had given to Myra regarding the impossibility of marriage between them. He had said all the things which he knew others might be expected to say; he had mercilessly expressed what would have been his own judgment had he been asked to pronounce an opinion concerning any other man and woman in like circumstances. As he voiced them they had sounded tragically plausible and stoically just. He knew he was inflicting almost unbearable pain upon himself and upon the woman whose whole love was his; but that pain seemed necessary to the tragic demands of the entire ghastly situation.

Only after he had finally left her and was on his way back to town, did Jim Airth realise that the pain he had thus inflicted upon her and upon himself, had been a solace to his own wounded pride. His had been the mistake, and it re-established him in his own self-respect and sense of superiority, that his should be the decision, so hard to make—so unfalteringly made—bringing down upon his own head a punishment out of all proportion to the fault committed.

But, now that the strain and tension were over, his natural honesty of mind reasserted itself, forcing him to admit that his own selfish pride had been at the bottom of his high-flown tragedy.

Myra's simple loving view of the case had been the right one; yet, thrusting it from him, he had ruthlessly plunged himself and her into a hopeless abyss of needless suffering.

By degrees he slowly realised that in so doing he had

deliberately inflicted a more cruel wrong upon the woman he loved, than that which he had unwittingly done her in the past.

Remorse and regret gnawed at his heart, added to an almost unbearable hunger for Myra. Yet he could not bring himself to return to her with this second and still more humiliating confession of failure.

His one hope was that Myra would find their separation impossible to endure, and would send for him. But the days went by, and Myra made no sign. She had said she would never send for him unless assured that coming to her would mean happiness to him. To this decision she quietly adhered.

In a strongly virile man, love towards a woman is, in its essential qualities, naturally selfish. Its keynote is, "I need"; its dominant, "I want"; its full major chord, "I must possess."

On the other hand, the woman's love for the man is essentially unselfish. Its keynote is, "He needs"; its dominant, "I am his, to do with as he pleases"; its full major chord, "Let me give all." In the Book of Canticles, one of the greatest love-poems ever written, we find this truth exemplified; we see the woman's heart learning its lesson, in a fine crescendo of self-surrender. In the first stanza she says: "My Belovèd is mine, and I am his"; in the second, "I am my Belovèd's and he is mine." But in the third, all else is merged in the instinctive joy of giving: "I am my Belovèd's, and his desire is towards me."

This is the natural attitude of the sexes, designed by an all-wise Creator; but designed for a condition of ideal perfection. No perfect law could be framed for imperfection. Therefore, if the working out prove often a failure, the fault lies in the imperfection of the workers, not in the perfection of the law. In those rare cases where the love is ideal, the man's "I take" and the woman's "I give" blend into an ideal union, each completing and modifying the other. But where sin of any kind comes in, a false note has been struck in the divine harmony, and the grand chord of mutual love fails to ring true.

Into their perfect love, Jim Airth had introduced the discord of false pride. It had become the basis of his line of action, and their symphony of life, so beautiful at first in its sweet theme of mutual love and trust, now lost its harmony, and jarred into a hopeless jangle. The very fact that she faithfully adhered to her trustful unselfishness, acquiescing without a murmur in his decision, made readjustment the more impossible. Thus the weeks went by.

Jim Airth worked feverishly at his proofs; drinking and smoking, when he should have been eating and sleeping; going off suddenly, after two or three days of continuous sitting at his desk, on desperate bouts of violent exercise.

He walked down to Shenstone by night; sat, in bitterness of spirit under the beeches, surrounded by empty wicker chairs;—a silent ghostly garden-party!—watched the dawn break over the lake; prowled around the house where Lady Ingleby lay sleeping, and narrowly escaped arrest at the hands of Lady Ingleby's night-watchman; leaving for London by the first train in the morning, more sick at heart than when he started.

Another time he suddenly turned in at Paddington, took the train down to Cornwall, and astonished the Miss Murgatroyds by stalking into the coffee-room, the gaunt ghost of his old gay self. Afterwards he went off to Horseshoe Cove, climbed the cliff and spent the night on the ledge, dwelling in morbid misery on the wonderful memories with which that place was surrounded.

It was then that fresh hope, and the complete acceptance of a better point of view, came to Jim Airth.

As he sat on the ledge, hugging his lonely misery, he suddenly became strangely conscious of Myra's presence. It was as if the sweet wistful grey eyes, were turned upon him in the darkness; the tender mouth smiled lovingly, while the voice he knew so well asked in soft merriment, as under the beeches at Shenstone: "What has come to you, you dearest old boy?"

He had just put his hand into his pocket and drawn out his spirit-flask. He held it for a moment, while he listened, spellbound, to that whisper; then flung it away into the darkness, far down to the sea below. "Davy Jones may have it," he said, and laughed aloud; "who e'er he be!" It was the first time Jim Airth had laughed since that afternoon beneath the Shenstone beeches.

Then, with the sense of Myra's presence still so near him, he lay with his back to the cliff, his face to the moonlit sea. It seemed to him as if again he drew her, shaking and trembling but unresisting, into his arms, holding her there in safety until her trembling ceased, and she slept the untroubled sleep of a happy child.

All the best and noblest in Jim Airth awoke at that hallowed memory of faithful strength on his part, and trustful peace on hers.

"My God," he said, "what a nightmare it has been! And what a fool, I, to think anything could come between us. Has she not been utterly mine since that sacred night spent here? And I have left her to loneliness and grief?.... I will arise and go to my belovèd. No past, no shame, no pride of mine, shall come between us any more."

He raised himself on his elbow and looked over the edge. The moonlight shone on rippling water lapping the foot of the cliff. He could see his watch by its bright light. Midnight! He must wait until

107

three, for the tide to go down. He leaned back again, his arms folded across his chest; but Myra was still safely within them.

Two minutes later, Jim Airth slept soundly.

The dawn awoke him. He scrambled down to the shore, and once again swam up the golden path toward the rising sun.

As he got back into his clothes, it seemed to him that every vestige of that black nightmare had been left behind in the gay tossing waters.

On his way to the railway station, he passed a farm. The farmer's wife had been up since sunrise, churning. She gladly gave him a simple breakfast of home-made bread, with butter fresh from the churn.

He caught the six o'clock express for town; tubbed, shaved, and lunched, at his Club.

At a quarter to three he was just coming down the steps into Piccadilly, very consciously "clothed and in his right mind," debating which train he could take for Shenstone if—as in duty bound—he looked in at his publishers' first; when a telegraph boy dashed up the steps into the Club, and the next moment the hall-porter hastened after him with a telegram.

Jim Airth read it; took one look at his watch; then jumped headlong into a passing taxicab.

"Charing Cross!" he shouted to the chauffeur. "And a sovereign if you do it in five minutes."

As the flag tinged down, and the taxi glided swiftly forward into the whirl of traffic, Jim Airth unfolded the telegram and read it again.

It had been handed in at Shenstone at ..

Come to me at once.

Myra.

A shout of exultation arose within him.

CHAPTER XXI

MICHAEL VERITAS

On the morning of that day, while Jim Airth, braced with a new resolve and a fresh outlook on life, was speeding up from Cornwall, Lady Ingleby sat beneath the scarlet chestnuts, watching Ronald and Billy play tennis.

They had entered for a tournament, and discovered that they required constant practice such as, apparently, could only be obtained at Shenstone. In reality they came over so frequently in honest-hearted trouble and anxiety over their friend, of whose unexpected sorrow they chanced to be the sole confidants. Lady Ingleby refused herself to all other visitors. In the trying uncertainty of these few weeks while Jim Airth was still in England, she dreaded questions or comments. To Jane Dalmain she had written the whole truth. The Dalmains were at Worcester, attending a musical festival in that noblest of English cathedrals; but they expected soon to return to Overdene, when Jane had promised to come to her.

Meanwhile Ronald and Billy turned up often, doing their valiant best to be cheerful; but Myra's fragile look, and large pathetic eyes, alarmed and horrified them. Obviously things had gone more hopelessly wrong than they had anticipated. They had known at once that Airth would not marry Lady Ingleby; but it had never occurred to them that Lady Ingleby would still wish to marry Airth. Ronald stoutly denied that this was the case; but Billy affirmed it, though refusing to give reasons.

Ronald had never succeeded in extorting from Billy one word of what had taken place when he had told Lady Ingleby that Jim Airth was the man.

"If you wanted to know how she took it, you should have told her yourself," said Billy. "And it will be a saving of useless trouble, Ron, if you never ask me again."

Thus the days went by; and, though she always seemed gently pleased to see them both, no possible opening had been given to Ronald for assuming the rôle of manly comforter.

"I shall give it up," said Ronnie at last, in bitterness of spirit; "I tell you, I shall give it up; and marry the duchess!"

"Don't be profane," counselled Billy. "It would be more to the point to find Airth, and explain to him, in carefully chosen language, that letting Lady Ingleby die of a broken heart will not atone for blowing up her husband. I always knew our news would make no difference, from the moment I saw her go quite pink when she told us his name. She never went pink over Ingleby, you bet! I didn't know they could do it, after twenty."

"Much you know, then!" ejaculated Ronnie, scornfully. "I've seen the duchess go pink."

"Scarlet, you mean," amended Billy. "So have I, old chap; but that's another pair o' boots, as you very well know."

"Oh, don't be vulgar," sighed Ronnie, wearily. "Let's cut the whole thing and go to town. Henley begins to-morrow."

But next day they turned up at Shenstone, earlier than usual.

And that morning, Lady Ingleby was feeling strangely restful and at peace; not with any expectations of future happiness; but resigned to the inevitable; and less apart from Jim Airth. She had fallen asleep the night before beset by haunting memories of Cornwall and of their climb up the cliff. At midnight she had awakened with a start, fancying herself on the ledge, and feeling that she was falling. But instantly Jim Airth's arms seemed to enfold her; she felt herself drawn into safety; then that exquisite sense of strength and rest was hers once more.

So vivid had been the dream, that its effect remained with her when she rose. Thus she sat watching the tennis with a little smile of content on her sweet face.

"She is beginning to forget," thought Ronnie, exultant. "My 'vantage!" he shouted significantly to Billy, over the net.

"Deuce!" responded Billy, smashing down the ball with unnecessary violence.

"No!" cried Ronnie. "Outside, my boy! Game and a 'love' set to me!"

"Stay to lunch, boys," said Lady Ingleby, as the gong sounded; and they all three went gaily into the house.

As they passed through the hall afterwards, their motor stood at the door; so they bade her good-bye, and turned to find their rackets.

At that moment they heard the sharp ting of a bicycle bell. A boy had ridden up with a telegram. Groatley, waiting to see them off, took it; picked up a silver salver from the hall table, and followed Lady Ingleby to her sitting-room.

There seemed so sudden a silence in the house, that Ronald and Billy with one accord stood listening.

"Twenty minutes to two," said Billy, glancing at the clock. "Spirits are walking."

The next moment a cry rang out from Lady Ingleby's sitting-room—a cry of such mingled bewilderment, wonder, and relief, that

110

they looked at one another in amazement. Then without waiting to question or consider, they hastened to her.

Lady Ingleby was standing in the middle of the room, an open telegram in her hand.

"Jim," she was saying; "Oh, Jim!"

Her face was so transfigured by thankfulness and joy, that neither Ronald nor Billy could frame a question. They merely gazed at her.

"Oh, Billy! Oh, Ronald!" she said, "He didn't do it! Oh think what this will mean to Jim Airth. Stop the boy! Quick! Bring me a telegram form. I must send for him at once.... Oh, Jim, Jim!.... He said he would give his life for the relief of the moment when some one should step into the tent and tell him he had not done it; and now I shall be that 'some one'!.... Oh, how do you spell 'Piccadilly'.... Please call Groatley. If we lose no time, he may catch the three o'clock express.... Groatley, tell the boy to take this telegram and have it sent off immediately. Give him half-a-crown, and say he may keep the change.... Now boys.... Shut the door!"

The whirlwind of excitement was succeeded by sudden stillness. Lady Ingleby sank upon the sofa, burying her face for a moment in the cushions.

In the silence they heard the telegraph boy disappearing rapidly into the distance, ringing his bell a very unnecessary number of times. When it could be heard no longer, Lady Ingleby lifted her head.

"Michael is alive," she said.

"Great Scot!" exclaimed Ronnie, and took a step forward.

Billy made no sound, but he turned very white; backed to the door, and leaned against it for support.

"Think what it means to Jim Airth!" said Lady Ingleby. "Think of the despair and misery through which he passed; and, after all, he had not done it."

"May we see?" asked Ronald eagerly, holding out his hand for the telegram.

Billy licked his dry lips, but no sound would come.

"Read it," said Myra.

Ronald took the telegram and read it aloud.

"*To Lady Ingleby, Shenstone Park, Shenstone, England.*

"*Reported death a mistake. Taken prisoner Targai. Escaped. Arrived Cairo. Large bribes and rewards to pay. Cable five hundred pounds to Cook's immediately.*

"*Michael Veritas.*"

"Great Scot!" said Ronnie again.

Billy said nothing; but his eyes never left Lady Ingleby's radiant face.

"Think what it will mean to Jim Airth," she repeated.

"Er—yes," said Ronnie. "It considerably changes the situation—for him. What does 'Veritas' mean?"

"That," replied Lady Ingleby "is our private code, Michael's and mine. My mother once wired to me in Michael's name, and to Michael in mine—dear mamma occasionally does eccentric things—and it made complications. Michael was very much annoyed; and after that we took to signing our telegrams 'Veritas,' which means: 'This is really from me.'"

"Just think!" said Ronnie. "He, a prisoner; and we, all marching away! But I remember now, we always suspected prisoners had been taken at Targai. And positive proofs of Lord Ingleby's death were difficult to—well, don't you know—to find. I mean—there couldn't be a funeral. We had to conclude it, because we believed him to have been right inside the tunnel. He must have got clear after all, before Airth sent the flash, and getting in with the first rush, been unable to return. Of course he has reached Cairo with no money and no means of getting home. And the chaps who helped him, will stick to him like leeches till they get their pay. What shall you do about cabling?"

Lady Ingleby seemed to collect her thoughts with difficulty.

"Of course the money must be sent—and sent at once," she said. "Oh, Ronnie, could you go up to town about it, for me? I would give you a cheque, and a note to my bankers; they will know how to cable it through. Could you, Ronnie? Michael must not be kept waiting; yet I must stay here to tell Jim. It never struck me that I might have gone up to town myself; and now I have wired to Jim to come down here. Oh, my dear Ronnie, could you?"

"Of course I could," said Ronald, cheerfully. "The motor is at the door. I can catch the two-thirty, if you write the note at once. No need for a cheque. Just write a few lines authorising your bankers to send out the money; I will see them personally; explain the whole thing, and hurry them up. The money shall be in Cairo to-night, if possible."

Lady Ingleby went to her davenport.

No sound broke the stillness save the rapid scratching of her pen.

Then Billy spoke. "I will come with you," he said, hoarsely.

"Why do that?" objected Ronald. "You may as well go on in the motor to Overdene, and tell them there."

"I am going to town," said Billy, decidedly. Then he walked

112

over to where the telegram still lay on the table. "May I copy this?" he asked of Lady Ingleby.

"Do," she said, without looking round.

"And Ronnie—you take the original to show them at the bank. Ah, no! I must keep that for Jim. Here is paper. Make two copies, Billy."

Billy had already copied the message into his pocket-book. With shaking fingers he copied it again, handing the sheet to Ronald, without looking at him.

The note written, Lady Ingleby rose.

"Thank you, Ronald," she said. "Thank you, more than I can say. I think you will catch the train. And good-bye, Billy."

But Billy was already in the motor.

CHAPTER XXII

LORD INGLEBY'S WIFE

The journey down from town had been as satisfactorily rapid as even Jim Airth could desire. He had caught the train at Charing Cross by five seconds.

The hour's run passed quickly in glowing anticipation of that which was being brought nearer by every turn of the wheels.

Myra's telegram was drawn from his pocket-book many times. Each word seemed fraught with tender meaning, "Come to me at once." It was so exactly Myra's simple direct method of expression. Most people would have said, "Come here," or "Come to Shenstone," or merely "Come." "Come to me" seemed a tender, though unconscious, response to his resolution of the night before: "I will arise and go to my belovèd."

Now that the parting was nearly over, he realised how terrible had been the blank of three weeks spent apart from Myra. Her sweet personality was so knit into his life, that he needed her—not at any particular time, or in any particular way—but always; as the air he breathed; or as the light, which made the day.

And she? He drew a well-worn letter from his pocket-book— the only letter he had ever had from Myra.

"I shall always want you," it said; "but I could never send, unless the coming would mean happiness for you."

Yet she had sent. Then she had happiness in store for him. Had she instinctively realised his change of mind? Or had she gauged his desperate hunger by her own, and understood that the satisfying of that, must mean happiness, whatever else of sorrow might lie in the background?

But there should be no background of anything but perfect joy, when Myra was his wife. Would he not have the turning of the fair leaves of her book of life? Each page should unfold fresh happiness, hold new surprises as to what life and love could mean. He would know how to guard her from the faintest shadow of disillusion. Even now it was his right to keep her from that. How much, after all, should he tell her of the heart-searchings of these wretched weeks? Last night he had meant to tell her everything; he had meant to say: "I have sinned against heaven—the heaven of our love—and before thee; and am no more worthy...." But was it not essential to a woman's happiness to believe the man she loved, to be in all ways, worthy? Out of his pocket came again the well-worn letter. "I know you decided as you felt right," wrote Myra. Why perplex her with explanations? Let the dead past bury its dead. No need to cloud, even momentarily, the joy with which they could now go forward into a new life. And what a life! Wedded life with Myra—

"Shenstone Junction!" shouted a porter and Jim Airth was across the platform before the train had stopped.

The tandem ponies waited outside the station, and this time Jim Airth gathered up the reins with a gay smile, flicking the leader, lightly. Before, he had said: "I never drive other people's ponies," in response to "Her ladyship's" message; but now—"All that's mine, is thine, laddie."

He whistled "Huntingtower," as he drove between the hayfields. Sprays of overhanging traveller's-joy brushed his shoulder in the narrow lanes. It was good to be alive on such a day. It was good not to be leaving England, in England's most perfect weather.... Should he take her home to Scotland for their honeymoon, or down to Cornwall?

What a jolly little church!

Evidently Myra never slacked pace for a gate. How the ponies dashed through, and into the avenue!

Poor Mrs. O'Mara! It had been difficult to be civil to her, when she had appeared instead of Myra to give him tea.

Of course Scotland would be jolly, with so much to show her; but Cornwall meant more, in its associations. Yes; he would arrange for the honeymoon in Cornwall; be married in the morning, up in town; no fuss; then go straight down to the old Moorhead Inn. And after dinner, they would sit in the honeysuckle arbour, and——

Groatley showed him into Myra's sitting-room.

She was not there.

He walked over to the mantelpiece. It seemed years since that evening when, in a sudden fury against Fate, he had crashed his fists upon its marble edge. He raised his eyes to Lord Ingleby's portrait. Poor old chap! He looked so content, and so pleased with himself, and his little dog. But he must have always appeared more like Myra's father than her—than anything else.

On the mantelpiece lay a telegram. After the manner of leisurely country post-offices, the full address was written on the envelope. It caught Jim Airth's eye, and hardly conscious of doing so, he took it up and read it. "Lady Ingleby, Shenstone Park, England." He laid it down. "England?" he wondered, idly. "Who can have been wiring to her from abroad?"

Then he turned. He had not heard her enter; but she was standing behind him.

"Myra!" he cried, and caught her to his heart.

The rapture and relief of that moment were unspeakable. No words seemed possible. He could only strain her to him, silently, with all his strength, and realise that she was safely there at last.

Myra had lifted her arms, and laid them lightly about his neck, hiding her face upon his breast.... He never knew exactly when he began to realise a subtle change about the quality of her embrace; the woman's passionate tenderness seemed missing; it rather resembled the trustful clinging of a little child. An uneasy foreboding, for which he could not account, assailed Jim Airth.

"Kiss me, Myra!" he said, peremptorily, and she, lifting her sweet face to his, kissed him at once. But it was the pure loving kiss of a little child.

Then she withdrew herself from his embrace; and, standing back, he looked at her, perplexed. The light upon her face seemed hardly earthly.

"Oh, Jim," she said, "God's ways are wonderful! I have such news for you, my friend. I thank God, it came before you had gone beyond recall. And I, who had been the one, unwittingly, to add so terribly to the weight of the lifelong cross you had to bear, am privileged to be the one to lift it quite away. Jim—you did not do it!"

Jim Airth gazed at her in troubled amazement. Into his mind, involuntarily, came the awesome Scotch word "fey."

"I did not do what, dear?" he asked, gently, as if he were speaking to a little child whom he was anxious not to frighten.

"You did not kill Michael."

"What makes you think I did not kill Michael, dear?" questioned Jim Airth, gently.

"Because," said Myra, with clasped hands, "Michael is alive."

"Dearest heart," said Jim Airth, tenderly, "you are not well. These awful three weeks, and what went before, have been too much for you. The strain has upset you. I was a brute to go off and leave you. But you knew I did what I thought right at the time; didn't you, Myra? Only now I see the whole thing quite differently. Your view was the true one. We ought to have acted upon it, and been married at once."

"Oh, Jim," said Myra, "thank God we didn't! It would have been so terrible now. It must have been a case of 'Even there shall Thy hand lead me, and Thy right hand shall hold me.' In our unconscious ignorance, we might have gone away together, not knowing Michael was alive."

Beads of perspiration stood on Jim Airth's forehead.

"My darling, you are ill," he said, in a voice of agonised anxiety. "I am afraid you are very ill. Do sit down quietly on the couch, and let me ring. I must speak to the O'Mara woman, or

116

somebody. Why didn't the fools let me know? Have you been ill all these weeks?"

Myra let him place her on the couch; smiling up at him reassuringly, as he stood before her.

"You must not ring the bell, Jim," she said. "Maggie is at the Lodge; and Groatley would be so astonished. I am quite well."

He looked around, in man-like helplessness; yet feeling something must be done. A long ivory fan, of exquisite workmanship, lay on a table near. He caught it up, and handed it to her. She took it; and to please him, opened it, fanning herself gently as she talked.

"I am not ill, Jim; really dear, I am not. I am only strangely happy and thankful. It seems too wonderful for our poor earthly hearts to understand. And I am a little frightened about the future— but you will help me to face that, I know. And I am rather worried about little things I have done wrong. It seems foolish—but as soon as I realised Michael was coming home, I became conscious of hosts of sins of omission, and I scarcely know where to begin to set them right. And the worst of all is—Jim! we have lost little Peter's grave! No one seems able to locate it. It is so trying of the gardeners; and so wrong of me; because of course I ought to have planted it with flowers. And Michael would have expected a little marble slab, by now. But I, stupidly, was too ill to see to the funeral; and now Anson declares they put him in the plantation, and George swears it was in the shrubbery. I have been consulting Groatley who always has ideas, and expresses them so well, and he says: 'Choose a suitable spot, m' lady; order a handsome tomb; plant it with choice flowers; and who's to be the wiser, till the resurrection?' Groatley is always resourceful; but of course I never deceive Michael. Fancy little Peter rising from the shrubbery, when Michael had mourned for years over a marble tomb on the lawn! But it really is a great worry. They must all begin digging, and keep on until they find something definite. It will be good for the shrubbery and the plantation, like the silly old man in the parable—no, I mean fable—who pretended he had hidden a treasure. Oh, Jim, don't look so distressed. I ought not to pour out all these trivial things to you; but since I have known Michael is coming back, my mind seems to have become foolish and trivial again. Michael always has that effect upon me; because— though he himself is so great and clever—he really thinks trivial and unimportant things are a woman's vocation in life. But oh, Jim— Jim Airth—with you I am always lifted straight to the big things; and our big thing to-day is this:—that you never killed Michael. Do you remember telling me how, as you lay in your tent recovering from the fever, if some one could have come in and told you Michael

117

was alive and well, and that you had not killed him after all, you would have given your life for the relief of that moment? Well, I am that 'some one,' and this is the 'moment'; and when first I had the telegram I could think of nothing—absolutely nothing, Jim—but what it would be to you."

"What telegram?" gasped Jim Airth. "In heaven's name, Myra, what do you mean?"

"Michael's telegram. It lies on the mantelpiece. Read it, Jim."

Jim Airth turned, took up the telegram and drew it from the envelope with steady fingers. He still thought Myra was raving.

He read it through, slowly. The wording was unmistakable; but he read it through again. As he did so he slightly turned, so that his back was toward the couch.

The blow was so stupendous. He could only realise one thing, for the moment:—that the woman who watched him read it, must not as yet see his face.

She spoke.

"Is it not almost impossible to believe, Jim? Ronald and Billy were lunching here, when it came. Billy seemed stunned; but Ronnie was delighted. He said he had always believed the first men to rush in had been captured, and that no actual proofs of Michael's death had ever been found. They never explained to me before, that there had been no funeral. I suppose they thought it would seem more horrible. But I never take much account of bodies. If it weren't for the burden of having a weird little urn about, and wondering what to do with it, I should approve of cremation. I sometimes felt I ought to make a pilgrimage to see the grave. I knew Michael would have wished it. He sets much store by graves—all the Inglebys lie in family vaults. That makes it worse about Peter. Ronnie went up to town at once to telegraph out the money. Billy went with him. Do you think five hundred is enough? Jim?—Jim! Are you not thankful? Do say something, Jim."

Jim Airth put back the telegram upon the mantelpiece. His big hand shook.

"What is 'Veritas'?" he asked, without looking round.

"That is our private code, Jim; Michael's and mine. My mother once wired to me in Michael's name, and to him in mine—poor mamma often does eccentric things, to get her own way—and it made complications, Michael was very much annoyed. So we settled always to sign important telegrams 'Veritas,' which means: 'This is really from me.'"

"Then—your husband—is coming home to you?" said Jim Airth, slowly.

118

"Yes, Jim," the sweet voice faltered, for the first time, and grew tremulous. "Michael is coming home."

Then Jim Airth turned round, and faced her squarely. Myra had never seen anything so terrible as his face.

"You are mine," he said; "not his."

Myra looked up at him, in dumb sorrowful appeal. She closed the ivory fan, clasping her hands upon it. The unquestioning finality of her patient silence, goaded Jim Airth to madness, and let loose the torrent of his fierce wild protest against this inevitable—this unrelenting, fate.

"You are mine," he said, "not his. Your love is mine! Your body is mine! Your whole life is mine! I will not leave you to another man. Ah, I know I said we could not marry! I know I said I should go abroad. But you would have remained faithful to me; and I, to you. We might have been apart; we might have been lonely; we might have been at different ends of the earth; but—we should have been each other's. I could have left you to loneliness; but, by God, I will not leave you to another!"

Myra rose, moved forward a few steps and stood, leaning her arm upon the mantelpiece and looking down upon the bank of ferns and lilies.

"Hush, Jim," she said, gently. "You forget to whom you are speaking."

"I am speaking," cried Jim Airth, in furious desperation, "to the woman I have won for my own; and who is mine, and none other's. If it had not been for my pride and my folly, we should have been married by now—married, Myra—and far away. I left you, I know; but—by heaven, I may as well tell you all now—it was pride—damnable false pride—that drove me away. I always meant to come back. I was waiting for you to send; but anyhow I should have come back. Would to God I had done as you implored me to do! By now we should have been together—out of reach of this cursed telegram,—and far away!"

Myra slowly lifted her eyes and looked at him. He, blinded by pain and passion, failed to mark the look, or he might have taken warning. As it was, he rushed on, headlong.

Myra, very white, with eyelids lowered, leaned against the mantelpiece; slowly furling and unfurling the ivory fan.

"But, darling," urged Jim Airth, "it is not yet too late. Oh, Myra, I have loved you so! Our love has been so wonderful. Have I not taught you what love is? The poor cold travesty you knew before—that was not love! Oh, Myra! you will come away with me, my own belovèd? You won't put me through the hell of leaving you to another man? Myra, look at me! Say you will come."

Then Lady Ingleby slowly closed the fan, grasping it firmly in her right hand. She threw back her head, and looked Jim Airth full in the eyes.

"So this is your love," she said. "This is what it means? Then I thank God I have hitherto only known the 'cold travesty,' which at least has kept me pure, and held me high. What? Would you drag me down to the level of the woman you have scorned for a dozen years? And, dragging me down, would you also trail, with me, in the mire, the noble name of the man whom you have ventured to call friend? My husband may not have given me much of those things a woman desires. But he has trusted me with his name, and with his honour; he has left me, mistress of his home. When he comes back he will find me what he himself made me—mistress of Shenstone; he will find me where he left me, awaiting his return. You are no longer speaking to a widow, Lord Airth; nor to a woman left desolate. You are speaking to Lord Ingleby's wife, and you may as well learn how Lord Ingleby's wife guards Lord Ingleby's name, and defends her own honour, and his." She lifted her hand swiftly and struck him, with the ivory fan, twice across the cheek. "Traitor!" she said, "and coward! Leave this house, and never set foot in it again!"

Jim Airth staggered back, his face livid—ashen, his hand involuntarily raised to ward off a third blow. Then the furious blood surged back. Two crimson streaks marked his cheek. He sprang forward; with a swift movement caught the fan from Lady Ingleby's hands, and whirled it above his head. His eyes blazed into hers. For a moment she thought he was going to strike her. She neither flinched nor moved; only the faintest smile curved the corners of her mouth into a scornful question.

Then Jim Airth gripped the fan in both hands; with a twist of his strong fingers snapped it in half, the halves into quarters, and again, with another wrench, crushed those into a hundred fragments—flung them at her feet; and, turning on his heel, left the room, and left the house.

CHAPTER XXIII

WHAT BILLY KNEW

Ronald and Billy had spoken but little, as they sped to the railway station, earlier on that afternoon.

"Rummy go," volunteered Ronald, launching the tentative comment into the somewhat oppressive silence.

Billy made no rejoinder.

"Why did you insist on coming with me?" asked Ronald.

"I'm not coming with you," replied Billy laconically.

"Where then, Billy? Why so tragic? Are you going to leap from London Bridge? Don't do it Billy-boy! You never had a chance. You were merely a nice kid. I'm the chap who might be tragic; and see—I'm going to the bank to despatch the wherewithal for bringing the old boy back. Take example by my fortitude, Billy."

Billy's explosion, when it came, was so violent, so choice, and so unlike Billy, that Ronald relapsed into wondering silence.

But once in the train, locked into an empty first-class smoker, Billy turned a white face to his friend.

"Ronnie," he said, "I am going straight to Sir Deryck Brand. He is the only man I know, with a head on his shoulders."

"Thank you," said Ronnie. "I suppose I dandle mine on my knee. But why this urgent need of a man with his head so uniquely placed?"

"Because," said Billy, "that telegram is a lie."

"Nonsense, Billy! The wish is father to the thought! Oh, shame on you, Billy! Poor old Ingleby!"

"It is a lie," repeated Billy, doggedly.

"But look," objected Ronald, unfolding the telegram. "Here you are. 'Veritas.' What do you make of that?"

"Veritas be hanged!" said Billy. "It's a lie; and we've got to find out what damned rascal has sent it."

"But what possible reason have you to throw doubt on it?" inquired Ronald, gravely.

"Oh, confound you!" burst out Billy at last; "I picked up the pieces!"

A very nervous white-faced young man sat in the green leather armchair in Dr. Brand's consulting-room. He had shown the telegram, and jerked out a few incoherent sentences; after which Sir Deryck, by means of carefully chosen questions, had arrived at the main facts. He now sat at his table considering them.

Then, turning in his revolving-chair, he looked steadily at Billy.

"Cathcart," he said, quietly, "what reason have you for being so certain of Lord Ingleby's death, and that this telegram is therefore a forgery?"

Billy moistened his lips. "Oh, confound it!" he said. "I picked up the pieces!"

"I see," said Sir Deryck; and looked away.

"I have never told a soul," said Billy. "It is not a pretty story. But I can give you details, if you like."

"I think you had better give me details," said Sir Deryck, gravely.

So, with white lips, Billy gave them.

The doctor rose, buttoning his coat. Then he poured out a glass of water and handed it to Billy.

"Come," he said. "Fortunately I know a very cute detective from our own London force who happens just now to be in Cairo. We must go to Scotland Yard for his address, and a code. In fact we had better work it through them. You have done the right thing, Billy; and done it promptly; but we have no time to lose."

Twenty-four hours later, the doctor called at Shenstone Park. He had telegraphed his train requesting to be met by the motor; and he now asked the chauffeur to wait at the door, in order to take him back to the station.

"I could only come between trains," he explained to Lady Ingleby, "so you must forgive the short notice, and the peremptory tone of my telegram. I could not risk missing you. I have something of great importance to communicate."

The doctor waited a moment, hardly knowing how to proceed. He had seen Myra Ingleby under many varying conditions. He knew her well; and she was a woman so invariably true to herself, that he expected to be able to foresee exactly how she would act under any given combination of circumstances.

In this undreamed of development of Lord Ingleby's return, he anticipated finding her gently acquiescent; eagerly ready to resume again the duties of wifehood; with no thought of herself, but filled with anxious desire in all things to please the man who, with his whims and fancies, his foibles and ideas, had for nine months passed completely out of her life. Deryck Brand had expected to find Lady Ingleby in the mood of a typical April day, sunshine and showers rapidly alternating; whimsical smiles, succeeded by ready tears; then, with lashes still wet, gay laughter at some mistake of her own, or at incongruous behaviour on the part of her devoted but erratic household; speedily followed by pathetic anxiety over her

122

own supposed short-comings in view of Lord Ingleby's requirements on his return.

Instead of this charming personification of unselfish, inconsequent, tender femininity, the doctor found himself confronted by a calm cold woman, with hard unseeing eyes; a woman in whom something had died; and dying, had slain all the best and truest in her womanhood.

"Another man," was the prompt conclusion at which the doctor arrived; and this conclusion, coupled with the exigency of his own pressing engagements, brought him without preamble, very promptly to the point.

"Lady Ingleby," he said, "a cruel and heartless wrong has been done you by a despicable scoundrel, for whom no retribution would be too severe."

"I am perfectly aware of that," replied Lady Ingleby, calmly; "but I fail to understand, Sir Deryck, why you should consider it necessary to come down here in order to discuss it."

This most unexpected reply for a moment completely nonplussed the doctor. But rapid mental adjustment formed an important part of his professional equipment.

"I fear we are speaking at cross-purposes," he said, gently. "Forgive me, if I appear to have trespassed upon a subject of which I have no knowledge whatever. I am referring to the telegram received by you yesterday, which led you to suppose the report of Lord Ingleby's death was a mistake, and that he might shortly be returning home."

"My husband is alive," said Lady Ingleby. "He has telegraphed to me from Cairo, and I expect him back very soon."

For answer, Deryck Brand drew from his pocket-book two telegrams.

"I am bound to tell you at once, dear Lady Ingleby," he said, "that you have been cruelly deceived. The message from Cairo was a heartless fraud, designed in order to obtain money. Billy Cathcart had reason to suspect its genuineness, and brought it to me. I cabled at once to Cairo, with this result."

He laid two telegrams on the table before her.

"The first is a copy of one we sent yesterday to a detective out there. The second I received three hours ago. No one—not even Billy—has heard of its arrival. I have brought it immediately to you."

Lady Ingleby slowly lifted the paper containing the first message. She read it in silence.

Watch Cook's bank and arrest man personating Lord

Ingleby who will call for draft of money. Cable particulars promptly.

The doctor observed her closely as she laid down the first message without comment, and took up the second.

Former valet of Lord Ingleby's arrested. Confesses to despatch of fraudulent telegram. Cable instructions.

Lady Ingleby folded both papers and laid them on the table beside her. The calm impassivity of the white face had undergone no change.

"It must have been Walker," she said. "Michael always considered him a scamp and shifty; but I delighted in him, because he played the banjo quite excellently, and was so useful at parish entertainments. Michael took him abroad; but had to dismiss him on landing. He wrote and told me the fact, but gave no reasons. Poor Walker! I do not wish him punished, because I know Michael would think it was largely my own fault for putting banjo-playing before character. If Walker had written me a begging letter, I should most likely have sent him the money. I have a fatal habit of believing in people, and of wanting everybody to be happy."

Then, as if these last words recalled a momentarily forgotten wound, the stony apathy returned to voice and face.

"If Michael is not coming back," said Lady Ingleby, "I am indeed alone."

The doctor rose, and stood looking down upon her, perplexed and sorrowful.

"Is there not some one who should be told immediately of this change of affairs, Lady Ingleby?" he asked, gravely.

"No one," she replied, emphatically. "There is nobody whom it concerns intimately, excepting myself. And not many know of the arrival of yesterday's news. I wrote to Jane, and I suppose the boys told it at Overdene. If by any chance it gets into the papers, we must send a contradiction; but no explanation, please. I dislike the publication of wrong doing. It only leads to imitation and repetition. Beside, even a poor worm of a valet should be shielded if possible from public execration. We could not explain the extenuating circumstances."

"I do not suppose the news has become widely known," said the doctor. "Your household heard it, of course?"

"Yes," replied Lady Ingleby. "Ah, that reminds me, I must stop operations in the shrubbery and plantation. There is no object in little Peter having a grave, when his master has none."

124

This was absolutely unintelligible to the doctor; but at such times he never asked unnecessary questions, for his own enlightenment.

"So after all, Sir Deryck," added Lady Ingleby, "Peter was right."

"Yes," said the doctor, "little Peter was not mistaken."

"Had I remembered him, I might have doubted the telegram," remarked Lady Ingleby. "What can have aroused Billy's suspicions?"

"Like Peter," said the doctor, "Billy had, from the first, felt very sure. Do not mention to him that I told you the doubts originated with him. He is a sensitive lad, and the whole thing has greatly distressed him."

"Dear Billy," said Lady Ingleby.

The doctor glanced at the clock, and buttoned his coat. He had one minute to spare.

"My friend," he said, "a second time I have come as the bearer of evil tidings."

"Not evil," replied Myra, in a tone of hopeless sadness. "This is not a world to which we could possibly desire the return of one we love."

"There is nothing wrong with the world," said the doctor. "Our individual heaven or hell is brought about by our own actions."

"Or by the actions of others," amended Lady Ingleby, bitterly.

"Or by the actions of others," agreed the doctor. "But, even then, we cannot be completely happy, unless we are true to our best selves; nor wholly miserable, unless to our own ideals we become false. I fear I must be off; but I do not like leaving you thus alone."

Lady Ingleby glanced at the clock, rose, and gave him her hand.

"You have been more than kind, Sir Deryck, in coming to me yourself. I shall never forget it. And I am expecting Jane Champion—Dalmain, I mean; why do one's friends get married?— any minute. She is coming direct from town; the phaeton has gone to the station to meet her."

"Good," said the doctor, and clasped her hand with the strong silent sympathy of a man who, desiring to help, yet realises himself in the presence of a grief he is powerless either to understand or to assuage.

"Good—very good," he said, as he stepped into the motor, remarking to the chauffeur: "We have nine minutes; and if we miss the train, I must ask you to run me up to town."

And he said it a third time, even more emphatically, when he had recovered from his surprise at that which he saw as the motor flew down the avenue. For, after passing Lady Ingleby's phaeton

125

returning from the station empty excepting for a travelling coat and alligator bag left upon the seat, he saw the Honourable Mrs. Dalmain walking slowly beneath the trees, in earnest conversation with a very tall man, who carried his hat, letting the breeze blow through his thick rumpled hair. Both were too preoccupied to notice the motor, but as the man turned his haggard face toward his companion, the doctor saw in it the same stony look of hopeless despair, which had grieved and baffled him in Lady Ingleby's. The two were slowly wending their way toward the house, by a path leading down to the terrace.

"Evidently—the man," thought the doctor. "Well, I am glad Jane has him in tow. Poor souls! Providence has placed them in wise hands. If faithful counsel and honest plain-speaking can avail them anything, they will undoubtedly receive both, from our good Jane."

Providence also arranged that the London express was one minute late, and the doctor caught it. Whereat the chauffeur rejoiced; for he was "walking out" with Her ladyship's maid, whose evening off it chanced to be. The all-important events of life are apt to hang upon the happenings of one minute.

126

CHAPTER XXIV

MRS. DALMAIN REVIEWS THE SITUATION

"So you see, Jane," concluded Lady Ingleby, pathetically, "as Michael is not coming back, I am indeed alone."

"Loving Jim Airth as you do—" said Jane Dalmain.

"Did," interposed Lady Ingleby.

"Did, and do," said Jane Dalmain, "you would have been worse than alone if Michael had, after all, come back. Oh, Myra! I cannot imagine anything more unendurable, than to love one man, and be obliged to live with another."

"I should not have allowed myself to go on loving Jim," said Lady Ingleby.

"Rubbish!" pronounced Mrs. Dalmain, with forceful decision. "My dear Myra, that kind of remark paves the way for the devil, and is one of his favourite devices. More good women have been tripped by over-confidence in their ability to curb and to control their own affections, than by direct temptation to love where love is not lawful. Men are different; their temptations are not so subtle. They know exactly to what it will lead, if they dally with sentiment. Therefore, if they mean to do the right thing in the end, they keep clear of the danger at the beginning. We cannot possibly forbid ourselves to go loving, where love has once been allowed to reign supreme. I know you would not, in the first instance, have let yourself care for Jim Airth, had you not been free. But, once loving him, if so appalling a situation could have arisen as the unexpected return of your husband, your only safe and honourable course would have been to frankly tell Lord Ingleby: 'I grew to love Jim Airth while I believed you dead. I shall always love Jim Airth; but, I want before all else to be a good woman and a faithful wife. Trust me to be faithful; help me to be good.' Any man, worth his salt, would respond to such an appeal."

"And shoot himself?" suggested Lady Ingleby.

"I said 'man,' not 'coward,'" responded Mrs. Dalmain, with fine scorn.

"Jane, you are so strong-minded," murmured Lady Ingleby. "It goes with your linen collars, your tailor-made coats, and your big boots. I cannot picture myself in a linen collar, nor can I conceive of myself as standing before Michael and informing him that I loved Jim!"

Jane Dalmain laughed good-humouredly, plunged her large

hands into the pockets of her tweed coat, stretched out her serviceable brown boots and looked at them.

"If by 'strong-minded' you mean a wholesome dislike to the involving of a straightforward situation in a tangle of disingenuous sophistry, I plead guilty," she said.

"Oh, don't quote Sir Deryck," retorted Lady Ingleby, crossly. "You ought to have married him! I never could understand such an artist, such a poet, such an eclectic idealist as Garth Dalmain, falling in love with you, Jane!"

A sudden light of womanly tenderness illumined Jane's plain face. "The wife" looked out from it, in simple unconscious radiance.

"Nor could I," she answered softly. "It took me three years to realise it as an indubitable fact."

"I suppose you are very happy," remarked Myra.

Jane was silent. There were shrines in that strong nature too wholly sacred to be easily unveiled.

"I remember how I hated the idea, after the accident," said Myra, "of your tying yourself to blindness."

"Oh, hush," said Jane Dalmain, quickly. "You tread on sacred ground, and you forget to remove your shoes. From the first, the sweetest thing between my husband and myself has been that, together, we learned to kiss that cross."

"Dear old thing!" said Lady Ingleby, affectionately; "you deserved to be happy. All the same I never can understand why you did not marry Deryck Brand."

Jane smiled. She could not bring herself to discuss her husband, but she was very willing at this critical juncture to divert Lady Ingleby from her own troubles by entering into particulars concerning herself and the doctor.

"My dear," she said, "Deryck and I were far too much alike ever to have dovetailed into marriage. All our points would have met, and our differences gaped wide. The qualities which go to the making of a perfect friendship by no means always ensure a perfect marriage. There was a time when I should have married Deryck had he asked me to do so, simply because I implicitly trusted his judgment in all things, and it would never have occurred to me to refuse him anything he asked. But it would not have resulted in our mutual happiness. Also, at that time, I had no idea what love really meant. I no more understood love until—until Garth taught me, than you understood it before you met Jim Airth."

"I wish you would not keep on alluding to Jim Airth," said Myra, wearily. "I never wish to hear his name again. And I cannot allow you to suppose that I should ever have adopted your strong-minded suggestion, and admitted to Michael that I loved Jim. I

128

should have done nothing of the kind. I should have devoted myself to pleasing Michael in all things, and made myself—yes, Jane; you need not look amused and incredulous; though I don't wear collars and shooting-boots, I can make myself do things—I should have made myself forget that there was such a person in this world as the Earl of Airth and Monteith."

"Oh spare him that!" laughed Mrs. Dalmain. "Don't call the poor man by his titles. If he must be hanged, at least let him hang as plain Jim Airth. If one had to be wicked, it would be so infinitely worse to be a wicked earl, than wicked in any other walk of life. It savours so painfully of the 'penny-dreadful', or the cheap novelette. Also, my dear, there is nothing to be gained by discussing a hypothetical situation, with which you do not after all find yourself confronted. Mercifully, Lord Ingleby is not coming back."

"Mercifully!" exclaimed Lady Ingleby. "Really, Jane, you are crude beyond words, and most unsympathetic. You should have heard how tactfully the doctor broke it to me, and how kindly he alluded to my loss."

"My dear Myra," said Mrs. Dalmain, "I don't waste sympathy on false sentiment. And if Deryck had known you were already engaged to another man, instead of devoting to you four hours of his valuable time, he could have sent a sixpenny wire: 'Telegram a forgery. Accept heartfelt congratulations!'"

"Jane, you are brutal. And seeing that I have just told you the whole story of these last weeks, with the cruel heart-breaking finale of yesterday, I fail to understand how you can speak of me as engaged to another man."

Instantly Jane Dalmain's whole bearing altered. She ceased looking quizzically amused, and left off swinging her brown boot. She sat up, uncrossed her knees, and leaning her elbows upon them, held out her large capable hands to Lady Ingleby. Her noble face, grandly strong and tender, in its undeniable plainness, was full of womanly understanding and sympathy.

"Ah, my dear," she said, "now we must come to the crux of the whole matter. I have merely been playing around the fringe of the subject, in order to give you time to recover from the inevitable strain of the long and painful recital you have felt it necessary to make, in order that I might fully understand your position in all its bearings. The real question is this: Are you going to forgive Jim Airth?"

"I must never forgive him," said Lady Ingleby, with finality, "because, if I forgave him, I could not let him go."

"Why let him go, when his going leaves your whole life desolate?"

129

"Because," said Myra, "I feel I could not trust him; and I dare not marry a man whom I love as I love Jim Airth, unless I can trust him as implicitly as I trust my God. If I loved him less, I would take the risk. But I feel, for him, something which I can neither understand nor define; only I know that in time it would make him so completely master of me that, unless I could trust him absolutely—I should be afraid."

"Is a man never to be trusted again," asked Jane, "because, under sudden fierce temptation, he has failed you once?"

"It is not the failing once," said Myra. "It is the light thrown upon the whole quality of his love—of that kind of love. The passion of it makes it selfish—selfish to the degree of being utterly regardless of right and wrong, and careless of the welfare of its unfortunate object. My fair name would have been smirched; my honour dragged in the mire; my present, blighted; my future, ruined; but what did he care? It was all swept aside in the one sentence: 'You are mine, not his. You must come away with me.' I cannot trust myself to a love which has no standard of right and wrong. We look at it from different points of view. You see only the man and his temptation. I knew the priceless treasure of the love; therefore the sin against that love seems to me unforgivable."

Mrs. Dalmain looked earnestly at her friend. Her steadfast eyes were deeply troubled.

"Myra," she said, "you are absolutely right in your definitions, and correct in your conclusions. But your mistake is this. You make no allowance for the sudden, desperate, overwhelming nature of the temptation before which Jim Airth fell. Remember all that led up to it. Think of it, Myra! He stood so alone in the world; no mother, no wife, no woman's tenderness. And those ten hard years of worse than loneliness, when he fought the horrors of disillusion, the shame of betrayal, the bitterness of desertion; the humiliation of the stain upon his noble name. Against all this, during ten long years, he struggled; fought a manful fight, and overcame. Then—strong, hardened, lonely; a man grown to man's full heritage of self-contained independence—he met you, Myra. His ideals returned, purified and strengthened by their passage through the fire. Love came, now, in such gigantic force, that the pigmy passion of early youth was dwarfed and superseded. It seemed a new and untasted experience such as he had not dreamed life could contain. Three weeks of it, he had; growing in certainty, increasing in richness, every day; yet tempered by the patient waiting your pleasure, for eagerly expected fulfilment. Then the blow—so terrible to his sensibilities and to his manly pride; the horrible knowledge that his own hand had brought loss and sorrow to you, whom he would have

130

shielded from the faintest shadow of pain. Then his mistake in allowing false pride to come between you. Three weeks of growing hunger and regret, followed by your summons, which seemed to promise happiness after all; for, remember while you had been bringing yourself to acquiesce in his decision as absolutely final, so that the news of Lord Ingleby's return meant no loss to you and to him, merely the relief of his exculpation, he had been coming round to a more reasonable point of view, and realising that, after all, he had not lost you. You sent for him, and he came—once more aglow with love and certainty—only to hear that he had not only lost you himself, but must leave you to another man. Oh Myra! Can you not make allowance for a moment of fierce madness? Can you not see that the very strength of the man momentarily turned in the wrong direction, brought about his downfall? You tell me you called him coward and traitor? You might as well have struck him! Such words from your lips must have been worse than blows. I admit he deserved them; yet Saint Peter was thrice a coward and a traitor, but his Lord, making allowance for a sudden yielding to temptation, did not doubt the loyalty of his love, but gave him a chance of threefold public confession, and forgave him. If Divine Love could do this—oh, Myra, can you let your lover go out into the world again, alone, without one word of forgiveness?"

"How do I know he wants my forgiveness, Jane? He left me in a towering fury. And how could my forgiveness reach him, even supposing he desired it, or I could give it? Where is he now?"

"He left you in despair," said Mrs. Dalmain, "and—he is in the library."

Lady Ingleby rose to her feet.

"Jane! Jim Airth in this house! Who admitted him?"

"I did," replied Mrs. Dalmain, coolly. "I smuggled him in. Not a soul saw us enter. That was why I sent the carriage on ahead, when we reached the park gates. We walked up the avenue, turned down on to the terrace and slipped in by the lower door. He has been sitting in the library ever since. If you decide not to see him, I can go down and tell him so; he can go out as he came in, and none of your household will know he has been here. Dear Myra, don't look so distraught. Do sit down again, and let us finish our talk.... That is right. You must not be hurried. A decision which affects one's whole life, cannot be made in a minute, nor even in an hour. Lord Airth does not wish to force an interview, nor do I wish to persuade you to grant him one. He will not be surprised if I bring him word that you would rather not see him."

"Rather not?" cried Myra, with clasped hands. "Oh Jane, if

131

you could know what the mere thought of seeing him means to me, you would not say 'rather not,' but 'dare not.'"

"Let me tell you how we met," said Mrs. Dalmain, ignoring the last remark. "I reached Charing Cross in good time; stopped at the book stall for a supply of papers; secured an empty compartment, and settled down to a quiet hour. Jim Airth dashed into the station with barely one minute in which to take his ticket and reach the train. He tore up the platform, as the train began to move; had not time to reach a smoker; wrenched open the door of my compartment; jumped in headlong, and sat down upon my papers; turned to apologise, and found himself shut in alone for an hour with the friend to whom you had written weekly letters from Cornwall, and of whom you had apparently told him rather nice things—or, at all events things which led him to consider me trustworthy. He recognised me by a recent photograph which you had shown him."

"I remember," said Myra. "I kept it in my writing-case. He took it up and looked at it several times. I often spoke to him of you."

"He introduced himself with straightforward simplicity," continued Mrs. Dalmain, "and then—we neither of us knew quite how it happened—in a few minutes we were talking without reserve. I believe he felt frankness with me on his part might enable me, in the future, to be a comfort to you—you are his one thought; also, that if I interceded, you would perhaps grant him that which he came to seek—the opportunity to ask your forgiveness. Of course we neither of us had the slightest idea of the possibility that yesterday's telegram could be incorrect. He sails for America almost immediately, but could not bring himself to leave England without having expressed to you his contrition, and obtained your pardon. He would have written, but did not feel he ought, for your sake, to run the risk of putting explanations on to paper. Also I honestly believe it is breaking his heart, poor fellow, to feel that you and he parted forever, in anger. His love for you is a very great love, Myra."

"Oh, Jane," cried Lady Ingleby, "I cannot let him go! And yet—I cannot marry him. I love him with every fibre of my whole being, and yet I cannot trust him. Oh, Jane, what shall I do?"

"You must give him a chance," said Mrs. Dalmain, "to retrieve his mistake, and to prove himself the man we know him to be. Say to him, without explanation, what you have just said to me: that you cannot let him go; and see how he takes it. Listen, Myra. The unforeseen developments of the last few hours have put it into your power to give Jim Airth his chance. You must not rob him of it. Years ago, when Garth and I were in an apparently hopeless tangle

132

of irretrievable mistake, Deryck found us a way out. He said if Garth could go behind his blindness and express an opinion which he only could have given while he had his sight, the question might be solved. I need not trouble you with details, but that was exactly what happened, and our great happiness resulted. Now, in your case, Jim Airth must be given the chance to go behind his madness, regain his own self-respect, and prove himself worthy of your trust. Have you told any one of the second telegram from Cairo?"

"I saw nobody," said Lady Ingleby, "from the moment Sir Deryck left me, until you walked in."

"Very well. Then you, and Deryck, and I, are the only people in England who know of it. Jim Airth will have no idea of any change of conditions since yesterday. Do you see what that means, Myra?"

Lady Ingleby's pale face flushed. "Oh Jane, I dare not! If he failed again——"

"He will not fail," replied Mrs. Dalmain, with decision; "but should he do so, he will have proved himself, as you say, unworthy of your trust. Then—you can forgive him, and let him go."

"I cannot let him go!" cried Myra. "And yet I cannot marry him, unless he is all I have believed him to be."

"Ah, my dear, my dear!" said Mrs. Dalmain, tenderly. "You need to learn a lesson about married life. True happiness does not come from marrying an idol throned on a pedestal. Before Galatea could wed Pygmalion, she had to change from marble into glowing flesh and blood, and step down from off her pedestal. Love should not make us blind to one another's faults. It should only make us infinitely tender, and completely understanding. Let me tell you a shrewd remark of Aunt Georgina's on that subject. Speaking to a young married woman who considered herself wronged and disillusioned because, the honeymoon over, she discovered her husband not to be in all things absolutely perfect: 'Ah, my good girl,' said Aunt 'Gina, rapping the floor with her ebony cane; 'you made a foolish mistake if you imagined you were marrying an angel, when we have it, on the very highest authority, that the angels neither marry nor are given in marriage. Men and women, who are human enough to marry, are human enough to be full of faults; and the best thing marriage provides is that each gets somebody who will love, forgive, and understand. If you had waited for perfection, you would have reached heaven a spinster, which would have been, to say the least of it, dull—when you had had the chance of matrimony on earth! Go and make it up with that nice boy of yours, or I shall find him some pretty—' But the little bride, her anger dissolving in laughter and tears, had fled across the lawn in pursuit of a tall figure

133

in tweeds, stalking in solitary dudgeon towards the river. They disappeared into the boathouse, and soon after we saw them in a tiny skiff for two, and heard their happy laughter. 'Silly babies!' said Aunt 'Gina, crossly, 'they'll do it once too often, when I'm not there to spank them; and then there'll be a shipwreck! Oh, why did Adam marry, and spoil that peaceful garden?' Whereat Tommy, the old scarlet macaw, swung head downwards from his golden perch, with such shrieks of delighted laughter, mingled with appropriate profanity, that Aunt 'Gina's good-humour was instantly restored. 'Give him a strawberry, somebody!' she said; and spoke no more on things matrimonial."

Myra laughed. "The duchess's views are always refreshing. I wonder whether Michael and I made the mistake of not realising each other to be human; of not admitting there was anything to forgive, and therefore never forgiving?"

"Well, don't make it with Jim Airth," advised Mrs. Dalmain, "for he is the most human man I ever met; also the strongest, and one of the most lovable. Myra, there is nothing to be gained by waiting. Let me send him to you now; and, remember, all he asks or expects is one word of forgiveness."

"Oh, Jane!" cried Lady Ingleby, with clasped hands. "Do wait a little while. Give me time to think; time to consider; time to decide."

"Nonsense, my dear," said Mrs. Dalmain, "When but one right course lies before you, there can be no possible need for hesitation or consideration. You are merely nervously postponing the inevitable. You remind me of scenes we used to have in the out-patient department of a hospital in the East End of London, to which I once went for training. When patients came to the surgery for teeth extraction, and the pretty sympathetic little nurse in charge had got them safely fixed into the chair; as one of the doctors, prompt and alert, came forward with unmistakably business-like forceps ready, the terrified patient would exclaim: 'Oh, let the nurse do it! Let the nurse do it!' the idea evidently being that three or four diffident pulls by the nurse, were less alarming than the sharp certainty of one from the doctor. Now, my dear Myra, you have to face your ordeal. If it is to be successful there must be no uncertainty."

"Oh, Jane, I wish you were not such a decided person. I am sure when you were the nurse, the poor things preferred the doctors. I am terrified; yet I know you are right. And, oh, you dear, don't leave me! See me through."

"I am never away from Garth for a night, as you know," said Mrs. Dalmain. "But he and little Geoff went down to Overdene this

134

morning, with Simpson and nurse; so, if your man can motor me over during the evening, I will stay as long as you need me."

"Ah, thanks," said Lady Ingleby. "And now, Jane, you have done all you can for me; and God knows how much that means. I want to be quite alone for an hour. I feel I must face it out, and decide what I really intend doing. I owe it to Jim, I owe it to myself, to be quite sure what I mean to say, before I see him. Order tea in the library. Tell him I will see him; and, at the end of the hour, send him here. But, Jane—not a hint of anything which has passed between us. I may rely on you?"

"My dear," said Mrs. Dalmain, gently, "I play the game!"

She rose and stood on the hearthrug, looking intently at her husband's painting of Lord Ingleby.

"And, Myra," she said at last, "I do entreat you to remember, you are dealing with an unknown quantity. You have never before known intimately a man of Jim Airth's temperament. His love for you, and yours for him, hold elements as yet not fully understood by you. Remember this, in drawing your conclusions. I had almost said, Let instinct guide, rather than reason."

"I understand your meaning," said Lady Ingleby. "But I dare not depend upon either instinct or reason. I have not been a religious woman, Jane, as of course you know; but—I have been learning lately; and, as I learn, I try to practise. I feel myself to be in so dark and difficult a place, that I am trying to say, 'Even there shall Thy hand lead me, and Thy right Hand shall hold me.'"

"Ah, you are right," said Jane's deep earnest voice; "that is the best of all. God's hand alone leads surely, out of darkness into light."

She put a kind arm firmly around her friend, for a moment.

Then:—"I will send him to you in an hour," she said, and left the room.

Lady Ingleby was alone.

CHAPTER XXV

THE TEST

The door of Myra's sitting-room opened quietly, and Jim Airth came in.

She awaited him upon the couch, sitting very still, her hands folded in her lap.

The room seemed full of flowers, and of soft sunset light.

He closed the door, and came and stood before her.

For a few moments they looked steadily into one another's faces.

Then Jim Airth spoke, very low.

"It is so good of you to see me," he said. "It is almost more than I had ventured to hope. I am leaving England in a few hours. It would have been hard to go—without this. Now it will be easy."

She lifted her eyes to his, and waited in silence.

"Myra," he said, "can you forgive me?"

"I do not know, Jim," she answered, gently. "I want to be quite honest with you, and with myself. If I had cared less, I could have forgiven more easily."

"I know," he said. "Oh, Myra, I know. And I would not have you forgive lightly, so great a sin against our love. But, dear—if, before I go, you could say, 'I understand,' it would mean almost more to me, than if you said, 'I forgive.'"

"Jim," said Myra, gently, a tremor of tenderness in her sweet voice, "I understand."

He came quite near, and took her hands in his, holding them for a moment, with tender reverence.

"Thank you, dear," he said. "You are very good."

He loosed her hands, and again she folded them in her lap. He walked to the mantelpiece and stood looking down upon the ferns and lilies.

She marked the stoop of his broad shoulders; the way in which he seemed to find it difficult to hold up his head. Where was the proud gay carriage of the man who swung along the Cornish cliffs, whistling like a blackbird?

"Jim," she said, "understanding fully, of course I forgive fully, if it is possible that between you and me, forgiveness should pass. I have been thinking it over, since I knew you were in the house, and wondering why I feel it so impossible to say, 'I forgive you.' And, Jim—I think it is because you and I are so one that there is no room for such a thing as forgiveness to pass from me to you, or from you to me. Complete comprehension and unfailing love, take the place of what would be forgiveness between those who were less to each other."

He lifted his eyes, for a moment, full of a dumb anguish, which wrung her heart.

"Myra, I must go," he said, brokenly. "There was so much I had to tell you; so much to explain. But all need of this seems swept away by your divine tenderness and comprehension. All my life through I shall carry with me, deep hidden in my heart, these words of yours. Oh, my dear—my dear! Don't speak again! Let them be the last. Only—may I say it?—never let thoughts of me, sadden your fair life. I am going to America—a grand place for fresh beginnings; a land where one can work, and truly live; a land where earnest endeavour meets with fullest success, and where a man's energy may have full scope. I want you to think of me, Myra, as living, and working, and striving; not going under. But, if ever I feel like going under, I shall hear your dear voice singing at my shoulder, in the little Cornish church, on the quiet Sabbath evening, in the sunset: 'Eternal Father, strong to save,' ... And—when I think of you, my dear—my dear; I shall know your life is being good and beautiful every hour, and that you are happy with—" he lifted his eyes to Lord Ingleby's portrait; they dwelt for a moment on the kind quiet face— "with one of the best of men," said Jim Airth, bravely

He took a last look at her face. Silent tears stole slowly down it, and fell upon her folded hands.

A spasm of anguish shot across Jim Airth's set features.

"Ah, I must go," he said, suddenly. "God keep you, always."

He turned so quickly, that his hand was actually upon the handle of the door, before Myra reached him, though she sprang up, and flew across the room.

"Jim," she said, breathlessly. "Stop, Jim! Ah, stop! Listen! Wait!—Jim, I have always known—I told Jane so—that if I forgave you, I could not let you go." She flung her arms around his neck, as he stood gazing at her in dumb bewilderment. "Jim, my belovèd! I cannot let you go; or, if you go, you must take me with you. I cannot live without you, Jim Airth!"

For the space of a dozen heart-beats he stood silent, while she hung around him; her head upon his breast, her clinging arms about his neck.

Then a cry so terrible burst from him, that Myra's heart stood still.

"Oh, my God," he cried, "this is the worst of all! Have I, in falling, dragged her down? Now, indeed am I broken—broken. What

137

was the loss of my own pride, my own honour, my own self-esteem, to this? Have I soiled her fair whiteness; weakened the noble strength of her sweet purity? Oh, not this—my God, not this!"

He lifted his hands to his neck, took hers by the wrists, and forcibly drew them down, stepping back a pace, so that she must lift her head.

Then, holding her hands against his breast: "Lady Ingleby," he said, "lift your eyes, and look into my face."

Slowly—slowly—Myra lifted her grey eyes. The fire of his held her; she felt the strength of him mastering her, as it had often done before. She could scarcely see the anguish in his face, so vivid was the blaze of his blue eyes.

"Lady Ingleby," he said, and the grip of his hands on hers, tightened. "Lady Ingleby—we stood like this together, you and I, on a fast narrowing strip of sand. The cruel sea swept up, relentless. A high cliff rose in front—our only refuge. I held you thus, and said: 'We must climb—or drown.' Do you remember?—I say it now, again. The only possible right thing to do is steep and difficult; but we must climb. We must mount above our lower selves; away from this narrowing strip of dangerous sand; away from this cruel sea of fierce temptation; up to the breezy cliff-top, up to the blue above, into the open of honour and right and perfect purity. You stood there, until now; you stood there—brave and beautiful. I dragged you down—God forgive me, I brought you into danger—Hush! listen! You must climb again; you must climb alone; but when I am gone, your climbing will be easy. You will soon find yourself standing, safe and high, above these treacherous dangerous waters. Forgive me, if I seem rough." He forced her gently backwards to the couch. "Sit there," he said, "and do not rise, until I have left the house. And if ever these moments come back to you, Lady Ingleby, remember, the whole blame was mine.... Hush, I tell you; hush! And will you loose my hands?"

But Myra clung to those big hands, laughing, and weeping, and striving to speak.

"Oh, Jim—my Jim!—you can't leave me to climb alone, because I am all your own, and free to be yours and no other man's, and together, thank God, we can stand on the cliff-top where His hand has led us. Dearest—Jim, dearest—don't pull away from me, because I must cling on, until you have read these telegrams. Oh, Jim, read them quickly! QQQ Sir Deryck Brand brought them down from town this afternoon. And oh, forgive me that I did not tell you at once.... I wanted you to prove yourself, what I knew you to be, faithful, loyal, honourable, brave, the man of all men whom I trust; the man who will never fail me in the upward climb, until we stand

138

together beneath the blue on the heights of God's eternal hills.... Oh, Jim——"

Her voice faltered into silence; for Jim Airth knelt at her feet, his head in her lap, his arms flung around her, and he was sobbing as only a strong man can sob, when his heart has been strained to breaking point, and sudden relief has come.

Myra laid her hands, gently, upon the roughness of his hair. Thus they stayed long, without speaking or moving.

And in those sacred minutes Myra learned the lesson which ten years of wedded life had failed to teach: that in the strongest man there is, sometimes, the eternal child—eager, masterful, dependent, full of needs; and that, in every woman's love there must therefore be an element of the eternal mother—tender, understanding, patient; wise, yet self-surrendering; able to bear; ready to forgive; her strength made perfect in weakness.

At length Jim Airth lifted his head.

The last beams of the setting sun, entering through the western window, illumined, with a ray of golden glory, the lovely face above him. But he saw on it a radiance more bright than the reflected glory of any earthly sunset.

"Myra?" he said, awe and wonder in his voice. "Myra? What is it?"

And clasping her hands about his neck as he knelt before her, she drew his head to her breast, and answered:

"I have learnt a lesson, my belovèd; a lesson only you could teach. And I am very happy and thankful, Jim; because I know, that at last, I—even I—am ready for wifehood."

CHAPTER XXVI

"WHAT SHALL WE WRITE?"

The hall at the Moorhead Inn seemed very homelike to Jim Airth and Myra, as they stood together looking around it, on their arrival.

Jim had set his heart upon bringing his wife there, on the evening of their wedding day. Therefore they had left town immediately after the ceremony; dined en route, and now stood, as they had so often stood before when bidding one another good-night, in the lamp-light, beside the marble table.

"Oh, Jim dear," whispered Myra, throwing back her travelling cloak, "doesn't it all seem natural? Look at the old clock! Five minutes past ten. The Miss Murgatroyds must have gone up, in staid procession, exactly four minutes ago. Look at the stag's head! There is the antler, on the topmost point of which you always hung your cap."

"Myra——"

"Yes, dear. Oh, I hope the Murgatroyds are still here. Let's look in the book.... Yes, see! Here are their names with date of arrival, but none of departure. And, oh, dearest, here is 'Jim Airth,' as I first saw it written; and look at 'Mrs. O'Mara' just beneath it! How well I remember glancing back from the turn of the staircase, seeing you come out and read it, and wishing I had written it better. You can set me plenty of copies now, Jim."

"Myra!——"

"Yes, dear. Do you know I am going to fly up and unpack. Then I will come out to the honeysuckle arbour and sit with you while you smoke. And we need not mind being late; because the dear ladies, not knowing we have returned, will not all be sleeping with doors ajar. But oh Jim, you must—however late it is—plump your boots out into the passage, just for the fun of making Miss Susannah's heart jump unexpectedly."

"Myra! Oh, I say! My wife——"

"Yes, darling, I know! But I am perfectly certain 'Aunt Ingleby' is peeping out of her little office at the end of the passage; also, Polly has finished helping Sam place our luggage upstairs, and I can feel her, hanging over the top banisters! Be patient for just a little while, my Jim. Let's put our names in the visitors' book. What shall we write? Really we shall be obliged eventually to let them know who you are. Think what an excitement for the Miss Murgatroyds. But, just for once, I am going to write myself down by the name, of all others, I have most wished to bear."

So, smiling gaily up at her husband, then bending over the table to hide her happy face from the adoration of his eyes, the newly-made Countess of Airth and Monteith took up the pen; and, without pausing to remove her glove, wrote in the visitors' book of the Moorhead Inn, in the clear bold handwriting peculiarly her own: